Our Sexual Manifesto

An Erotic Novella Series

Book 1

First Breath

AJ Bradley

Table of Contents and Timeline

Preface

Wednesday, November 13, 2001

It was 6:00 am when Gweneth Cooper walked in the door of her studio apartment in Hollywood, FL. She set her keys on a gray formica countertop that separated the bedroom from the kitchen, dropped the non-designer gym bag on the floor, and fell onto her bed.

Nothing woke her for the next fourteen hours. Several missed phone calls and a knock at the door went completely unheard. Gweneth opened her eyes just after 8:00 pm and felt as if she had been dreaming for days.

It was normally dark outside when Gweneth got out of bed and started her usual morning routine. After taking a shower and a few minutes of basic makeup application Gweneth normally sees the morning sun peeking over the horizon, providing a glimpse of natural light.

This time she walked out of the bathroom to a very dark room and she completely froze. "What time is it?" Gweneth asked herself out loud.

Gweneth turned on the light switch next to the front door and looked at the clock on the stove, microwave, and alarm clock. All read 8:46. Gweneth started searching through her gym bag and found her cell phone. She flipped up the earpiece and read the bright screen.

Wednesday 11/13/2001. 8:47 pm.

Gweneth sat on the side of her bed and tried not to panic. Her last solid memory was Monday afternoon. She left work early for a job interview on South Beach. She didn't remember the interview, and her next memory was walking into her apartment and going straight to bed. She didn't remember going to work Tuesday or Wednesday and can't believe she slept for two whole days.

Gweneth looked up and saw the number six flashing on her answering machine. She pressed play and the messages started:

"First message, left Tuesday at 8:19 am: 'Gwen, it's Todd from work. We were expecting you at eight this morning, and we haven't heard from you. I hope you're feeling ok. Let us know if you'll be in. Thanks.'"

"Next message, left Tuesday at 1:40 pm: 'Gwen, this is Robin Jacobson from Human Resources. We have not heard from you and since you did not call, we have recorded this as a no-call no-show. Please contact this office as soon as possible. Thank you.'"

"Next message, left Tuesday at 7:05 pm: 'Babe, I haven't heard from you all day. Please answer the phone. I've left a message on your cell and home phone now. Please call me when you get this.'"

"Next message, left today at 8:15 am: 'Gwen, it's Todd from work again. Did you quit and not tell anyone? I would have thought you would have told me. I'm not mad or anything but it's just kind of weird not having you here. Call me back if you want to. Hope to see you.'"

"Next message, left today at 11:35 am: 'Gwen this is Robin from HR. We haven't heard from you since Monday so we are left with no choice but to terminate your employment with our company. You may pick up your personal belongings from the security desk until Friday. Please turn in your parking permit at the security desk as well. Wish you the best with your future endeavors.'"

"Next message, left today at 4:21 pm: 'Gwen, it's Scott. I'm not playing these games. If you're not going to talk to me, then I think it's best that we move on. Sorry to do this on your machine, but I feel that's why you're dodging my calls. I hope you find what you're looking for.'"

Gweneth sat in silence, petrified about what had happened. She felt ok, and had no signs of struggle or bruises. Other than being very disoriented and confused she physically felt great. She remembered having plans with a few friends after her interview but couldn't remember what they did. Numerous scenarios raced through her mind, the first one she thought of was if she was roofied or drugged?

Gweneth looked out her window and could see her car in her normal spot. She vaguely remembers driving home but wasn't concerned with if she was *ok* to drive.

Gweneth felt her first panic attack coming on. She felt fear and anxiety building with every second she sat in her apartment.

She looked at her gym bag on the floor next to her bed. She opened the gym bag and started sorting the contents. Nothing was missing, although she found an empty check envelope which wasn't there before. This was reassuring and perpetuated her panic at the same time.

'Maybe there's a clue in the car?' Gweneth thought to herself. She grabbed her keys off the counter and jogged out to her 1993 Honda Civic. She opened the driver's door and sat down. Everything was in its place and there were no signs of anything bad happening. Gweneth kept a very tidy apartment which carried over to her car.

Gweneth felt fear start to rise again as she fought to hold back tears. She had lost her memory of the last two days; her job, and her boyfriend, with no clues, explanations, or reasons as to why she couldn't remember.

As the tears started rolling down her cheeks Gweneth found herself breathing rhythmically. One deep breath in through her mouth and then a very slow exhale out the nose. She took another deep breath, deeper than the previous breath, and noticed her diaphragm expanding and contracting.

The fear and panic subsided enough for her to think about lowering the sunshade to access the mirror on the back. A small piece of paper, folded twice, fell into her lap along with an ATM receipt.

She didn't have any memory of putting that piece of paper there and began to unfold it. The first fold revealed her handwriting and three numbered notes:

1. My Vision of who I want to be.
2. My health, wealth, and self.
3. My Sister and Mother.

Gweneth felt the note seemed familiar. She recognized her own handwriting and looking at it felt like recalling a dream. For a moment, Gweneth wondered if she was still dreaming. She could tell there was something else written on the inside of the paper. Gweneth unfolded the rest to reveal only one word.

REMEMBER

She read it several times. 'Remember what?' Gweneth thought to herself as she turned the piece of paper over and noticed it was written on hotel stationery from the Ritz-Carlton South Beach.

Gweneth then looked at the ATM receipt. She didn't remember going to the ATM and was curious what she withdrew money for. As she unfolded it her jaw dropped. The receipt didn't show a withdrawal but a deposit for $20,000. The account number on the receipt was hers and the date and time showed earlier that morning. 11/13/01 5:47 am.

A flood of questions and anxiety swept over Gweneth. She now knew she had been at the Ritz Carlton South Beach. She was also at the bank just fifteen hours ago. How she came to deposit $20,000 was causing her the most anxiety and she looked back at the note accompanying the ATM receipt.

REMEMBER

After several minutes Gweneth realized she was still breathing in rhythm. She felt less anxious and was starting to remember pieces of the evening. This was now a mission and mystery she

was confident had a solution. It started to rain, which is common for south Florida. Gweneth put the note and ATM receipt in her pocket, locked her car, and jogged back to her apartment.
Once inside, she went straight to the kitchen and started preparing a single cup of coffee. Gweneth pulled the note from her pocket and looked at the word REMEMBER, and said it out loud several times. "Remember...Remember...Remember what?"

She added sugar and lactose-free creamer to her coffee, walked over to her desk, and turned on her desktop computer. Knowing it would be a few minutes before her computer would be usable, Gweneth walked into the bathroom. She washed her hands, splashed cool water on her face, and took a deep breath. Gweneth realized she was no longer breathing in rhythm. She started again, this time consciously, by taking a deep breath in through her mouth, down into the pit of her stomach, and then a slow controlled exhale through her nose. She could immediately feel a difference in how she felt and how she thought.

Gweneth closed her eyes and took another breath, slow exhale, another breath, slow exhale. After five repetitions Gweneth opened her eyes and looked at her reflection. What she saw was familiar like a dream, just like the note in the car.

Gweneth leaned closer to the mirror and looked into her own eyes, to make sure it was actually her. She involuntarily took a long breath in through her nose and exhaled with a loud sigh. Gweneth refocused on her reflection but couldn't figure out how it was different. She realized her reflection was smiling back at her, however, Gweneth knew she wasn't smiling at all. Gweneth's reflection leaned closer and whispered, "Remember."
Gweneth's breathing changed immediately. It was much faster than before but still followed a pattern. She felt as if something or someone was controlling her. She walked quickly to her bed and laid down, still breathing very controlled, but fast and seemingly impossible to stop.

Within seconds of her head hitting the pillow, she started remembering, and for Gweneth, it was like experiencing a movie of memories.

CHAPTER 1
Miami, FL - 2001

Tuesday, November 12th
1:34 am

Joshua Miller stepped off the elevator on the fifth floor of the Ritz-Carlton Hotel on South Beach. It was just past 1:30 am and Joshua knew he was exhausted by how slowly he was walking to his room. He pulled his room key from his left pants pocket and dropped it immediately along with several coins and a piece of paper he had never seen before. Joshua went down to one knee, picked up what he had dropped, unfolded the unfamiliar piece of paper, which had one word neatly printed.

TONIGHT

Joshua knew what this message was and he could not have been more unprepared. The note he held in his hands was a signal that a series of tests had already been set in motion.
This was a test of balance, control, trust, and surrender. Joshua closed his eyes and took several deep and controlled breaths. He stood up, returned the note and coins to his pocket, then proceeded to his room not knowing what or who was waiting for him.

Joshua opened the door to room 5015 and immediately smelled tobacco, scented candles, and a familiar perfume that belonged to a beautiful young woman waiting for Joshua to arrive.
She lay naked on the bed with a lit cigarette in her hand, slowly exhaling and speaking with a very intoxicating voice.

"What are you most afraid of?" The young woman asked.

"Answering that question." Joshua replied.

Candlelight illuminated the crest of her hip and breast casting her stomach and everything south into shadows. She smiled the most beautiful smile and inhaled another drag from her cigarette. Joshua sat down in the chair across from the bed and relaxed for the first time all day. The young woman did not take offense with his choice of positioning or his body language, which was not helping set the mood. She introduced herself in a very sensual way.

"My name is Ashley."
She put her cigarette out in a hotel ashtray on the bed and sat up exposing herself to Joshua. "You're probably wondering what I'm doing in your bed?"

"Unless we're expecting someone else, I can imagine what you came for, what eludes me is why?" Joshua asked.
He recognized the young woman from earlier in the evening. She had introduced herself during the reception following an NLP seminar Joshua was the keynote speaker for.

"I don't think you should be asking why I'm here." Ashley replied, seductively putting the tip of her index finger on her bottom lip. "You should be asking yourself what you're going to do with me while I'm here."
It was obvious she was trying to seduce Joshua, however, it seemed she did not know the real reason she was there. Sometimes participants in such scenarios had no knowledge of their true purpose or what they were asked to do, if asked at all. In many cases, they were put under certain levels of hypnosis for several hours to be awakened afterward with no recollection of what they did or the role they played.

Ashley leaned back into the light, exposing a perfectly curved breast and a soft nipple. Her small 5'4" frame only took up a small portion of the king-sized bed that Joshua was most interested in sleeping in at this point.

"I was at the seminar tonight and saw your presentation." She paused then looked down and locked eyes with Joshua. "I was inspired by how passionate you are about your work. I knew immediately I needed to be alone with you. Just for one night."

Ashley paused and took a few controlled breaths, just as Joshua had done moments before entering the room. They were using a similar breathing pattern which Joshua noticed right away.
The young woman did not appear to be conscious of her controlled breathing which gave Joshua more insight. He knew this was a test for both of them. She didn't know why she was there but it was now Joshua's mission to understand why so he'd know how to proceed.

Ashley continued. "I can sense your passion with the way you speak. I needed to do something spontaneous and insane. So, here I am, ready and willing to completely give myself to you until morning."

"Wow, ah…." Joshua was speechless. He wanted to sleep more than anything and had an important workshop starting in six hours. He looked at the clock. It was almost two o'clock in the morning. He thought of the consequences of asking her to leave, or worse, failing his test. His career could be ruined and the life of his only daughter could be at stake.
Joshua realized he didn't have a choice. He also didn't know how long her conversion would take. He needed to break the current state of consciousness for this young woman in order to begin her reprogramming. He needed her to say her full first name, out loud.
"Ashley, what's your real name?' Joshua asked.

"Ashley. I told you already." She responded, trying to smile, and again started breathing rhythmically without decision.
Joshua looked deep into her eyes. He saw past the shell and the short-term hypnosis.

"What's your, ...*real* name?" He asked, soft and sensual and without breaking eye contact. Joshua spoke slowly, communicating more with his eyes than with his voice.

"Gwen." She replied, surprised by her own answer.

"Is that short for…?" Joshua asked, pushing a few strands of hair behind her ear.

"Gweneth, but only my grandparents called me that." She paused with a noticeable difference in breathing. Her breaths were no longer controlled and started becoming shallow.

Joshua knew the first layer was peeled back. He looked at Gweneth and made a very quick decision. He stood up, walked over to the door, and pulled it open. Gweneth looked disappointed and lowered her head as if surrendering defeat. Joshua saw what he was looking for in her body language.

"Gweneth, you have a confidence problem." Joshua stated boldly enough for her to lift her head and show a strong effort to hold back tears. "We have a lot of work to do."
He reached behind the door and moved the **Do Not Disturb** sign to the hallway and let the heavy door close on its own.
Joshua walked over to the chair he had been sitting on and picked up his phone on the desk.

"I have to make one quick call and then I want to hear about you." Joshua told Gweneth with the most sincerity in his voice he could muster. She smiled with a little more blush in her face than before.

"Do you want me to put my clothes back on?" Gweneth asked, no longer confident and seductive.

"Absolutely not." Joshua said, returning the smile. "Nudity helps rejuvenate purity."

Gweneth's expression changed to one of confusion when Paul Johnson answered his phone after the third ring.

"Hello." He paused to see who was calling. "Joshua? It's 2 a.m. What's going on?" Paul asked with concern in his voice.

"Paul, I'm sorry to wake you. I have to tell you something important, do you need a minute to wake up?" Joshua asked with real empathy in every word.

"What?" Paul asked. "No, boss. I'm awake, what's going on?"

"I'm canceling my workshop tomorrow. I need tomorrow completely cleared. We'll get back to work Wednesday. Do you understand?" Joshua was blunt and straightforward with Paul so there weren't any misunderstandings.

"What's wrong J? We can't clear tomorrow. Tomorrow is the biggest day yet. After tonight, tomorrow has so much momentum, it would take a hurricane to demolish half the state to stop tomorrow from happening."

Joshua could hear the pleading in Paul's voice. He knew Paul had worked just as hard and deserved the credit and opportunity. Joshua made a different decision, which for him was the harder decision to make.
"Paul, listen to me. I can't tell you why I can't be there tomorrow. There is something very important I have to take care of."

Joshua paused and looked directly at Gweneth.

"Paul, you're ready and I wouldn't put this on you if I thought you couldn't handle it. I need you to take the lead tomorrow and do whatever you have to do to accommodate who and what we need. Can you take care of this for me?" Joshua asked, very collected, calm, and confident.

"Boss, I would take a bullet for you, any day. But what you are asking of me is impossible. A lot of people will be upset." Paul

sighed. "Josh, I'll do what I can. I need you to promise me that Wednesday we will be leaving this hotel and moving on with our schedule."
Paul wasn't happy, and Joshua knew that because he knew what he was asking was momentous and very out of character for him. Paul also only called him Josh when he was upset. Otherwise, it was J, Joshua, or Mr. Miller.

"Paul, I will meet you downstairs at 6 a.m. Wednesday morning. You are a good friend to take on the burden of being mine." Joshua responded, sincere and grateful.

"I'm a great friend. Good night." Paul ended the call before Joshua which wasn't normal.

Joshua turned the power to his cell phone off and forwarded all the room calls to the voicemail box. He turned his focus back on Gweneth, now lying on her stomach, her eyes fixed on him.
"You asked me what I am afraid of? I just did it." Joshua stated. "Making that call and putting that big of a burden on one of my closest friends. Having to make that decision and deliver that news scares me more than anything. But it's something I needed to do."

Gweneth spoke, with a less penetrating voice. "Now I feel guilty. I'm only thinking about myself."

"Gweneth." Joshua said, calm and relaxed. "I don't want you to feel guilty for anything. I want you to release any anxiety you might have stored up in your body. By this time tomorrow Gweneth, you will feel like a completely different person."

Gweneth looked up with the most curious of glances. "What are we going to do?" She asked, carefully.

Joshua sat beside her on the bed. She lifted her head and made a small effort to cover her chest. He pushed her hair behind her ear again and smiled.

"I'm going to take a shower. I need to change and gather myself." Joshua said. "While I'm in the shower I want you to make yourself comfortable and write down the three most important things in your life."

Her curious look changed into one of disbelief and confusion. "I came here to seduce you and hope you would pounce on me. We'd have our fling, and off I go. I don't need to be purified or saved. I just wanted to take a risk and do something I would never do." Gweneth was justifying her internal thoughts of leaving.

Joshua stood up and started to take off his shirt. Gweneth rolled over and sat up on the other side of the bed. She reached down and grabbed her dress from the floor. She pulled it on and stood up, grabbing her panties as well.
"I'm sorry." Gweneth said, not sounding apologetic. "I think I made a big mistake. I should go and you can still keep your schedule for tomorrow. I think that would be best." She sighed, disappointed in herself for again, giving up.

"Gweneth." Joshua said gently but with strong masculinity. She looked up at him with vulnerable eyes and an expression of self-defeat.
"You are giving in to your fear right now. This is where your insecurities are." Joshua took her hand in his. Gweneth forced a small and brief smile but still looked defeated.
Joshua walked her around to the mirror in the room and stood behind her as she looked at their reflection. He took her right hand into his and raised her arm straight out and formed a fist with her fingers. He then raised her left arm in the same way and whispered in her ear.

"You are strong. You can see this through."

Joshua gently kissed the back of her neck. Gweneth closed her eyes as Joshua pulled her arms slowly back to her sides. His hands came up the back of her arms and rested on her shoulders and started to gently massage them as he whispered in her ear again.

"You are not afraid. Let all your anxiety and worry fall down and you won't ever have to pick them up."

Joshua slid his hands down her hips and wrapped them around her stomach, pulling her close. He moved his right hand over her breast, grazing her hardening nipple, and held it on her chest. Joshua took a deep breath with closed eyes and held Gweneth, hand over heart.

After another deep breath, Joshua felt Gweneth take the same type of breath and heard her sigh, the most gentle of sighs.

"That's what I needed to hear." Joshua whispered. "That was fear leaving your body. Take another deep breath, exhale, and don't hold back on the sigh."

Gweneth followed his instructions and released more tension in her back and shoulders. Joshua turned her around to face him as she opened her eyes and focused straight into his. He could see that she had pain from the past, but beyond the pain, he could see amazing ideas, abundant energy, and a soul stronger than most.

"Are you afraid?" Joshua asked.

"No." Gweneth replied without blinking her eyes. Joshua touched her cheek with his warm palm. He moved his left hand to the side of her neck and very slowly kissed her on the mouth with their eyes still open, locked on each other. The kiss was soft and lasted just under a minute, but for Gweneth, it felt like an hour.

She smiled and looked down, embarrassed. Joshua lifted her head by her chin and asked, "Do you know what we just did?"

Gweneth replied, "I normally refer to that as kissing. Don't you?"

"Actually, we performed the first step of a purity ritual practiced over a thousand years ago." Joshua explained. "By kissing with our eyes open, and exchanging breaths, we looked into each other's souls. If our souls were not compatible one of us would have had a vision or become extremely weak."

"What is this ritual you keep talking about?" Gweneth asked.

"I will explain more as we go, but the intent of the ritual is to restore purity to your soul and balance your sexual energy with your divine energy. In most cases, the ritual renders people reborn. It will be life-changing if you take it seriously and see it through till the end."

"This is not what I expected." Gweneth stated, still unsure of herself. "Will I remember any of this?"

"Yes. You will remember everything as well as some things you may have suppressed." Joshua stepped back and smiled. "Now, I need to go take a shower. Are you ok out here for a few minutes?"

"Yes. I'll be fine." Gweneth said.

Joshua picked up the hotel stationary on the desk and handed it to Gweneth with a pen. "Write down the three most important things in your life. Be honest with yourself and write them very clearly so that you remember why you chose them. You can put on some music. I have a case of CDs and a Discman on the side table."

Joshua disappeared into the bathroom to start the water for his shower. He peeked around the corner and saw Gweneth looking at herself in the mirror. He then closed the bathroom door, got into the shower, and stood underneath the water for a few minutes. Joshua was nervous about missing the workshop but was more nervous about the next twenty-six hours with Gweneth. It had been almost six months since he last had this opportunity and it was long overdue.

• • • •

Joshua stepped out of the shower and towel-dried his hair along with the rest of his body. Joshua was above average height but didn't consider himself tall at six feet even. He ate well and worked out when he could, which proved difficult being on the road twenty-two weeks a year. Joshua didn't use tobacco and rarely let alcohol get the better of him. He was more familiar with the effects of certain psychotropic compounds used in various healing practices around the world.

Joshua had good upper body strength and a lean build but was not six-pack ripped. More importantly, Joshua understood the psychological aspects of having a positive body image and he never felt self-conscious or embarrassed when nude.

He brushed his teeth with his eyes closed and was breathing in and out through his nose at a quicker pace than before. He then wrapped his lower body in the towel and stepped out into the room where he'd left Gweneth just ten minutes before. The candles were still lit, and the music playing was coming from a portable CD player connected to a pair of small portable speakers.

Gweneth was laying on the bed, wearing only her panties, and was halfway through another cigarette. She turned around and smiled at Joshua.

"I like this CD." She said, "I've never heard of this band, 'The Mighty, Mighty Bosstones.'"

"They're a newer band." Joshua replied as he walked over to the desk and started flipping through a small case of CDs. He found the one he was looking for and changed the music which immediately changed the mood.

"Did you write down the three most important things in your life?"

"I did."   Gweneth replied, handing Joshua the small hotel stationary and extinguishing her cigarette. Joshua took the paper, folded it without reading it, and set it on the nightstand.

"Are you going to read them?" Gweneth asked.

Joshua sat on the bed next to Gweneth and touched both of her shoulders with his warm hands. "I'll look at them soon enough."

He looked deep into Gweneth's eyes and smiled. He was reading her energy and he felt she was in a good place to start.
"I want to hear about you, Gweneth." Joshua said in a very sensual way while still making direct eye contact. Gweneth again started breathing in rhythm, unaware of her pattern change. "Do you enjoy receiving massages?" Joshua asked.

"I would love a massage if you're offering." Gweneth said as she smiled and rolled over exposing her perfectly crevassed back, smooth skin, and a small tattoo of an astrological sun just above her right butt cheek.

"I've noticed two separate times now where you've started breathing in a specific rhythm and I'm wondering if you're doing that consciously?" Joshua was probing how aware Gweneth was of the situation.

"I don't think so." Gweneth said. "Now that you mention it, that does sound really familiar."
"Nothing to worry about, I was just curious." Joshua replied, changing the subject quickly. "During the massage please keep breathing like you are. Deep breaths in through your nose and slow controlled exhales from your mouth."
Joshua retrieved an extra towel from the bathroom and a bottle of massage oil. He folded and draped the towel over Gweneth's bottom, then pulled a small glass vial from deep in his suitcase. He unscrewed the cap and with a dropper added six drops of solution to the body oil and tipped the bottle back and forth, mixing in what he had added.

"Gweneth." Joshua said slowly with deep masculinity in his voice. "I want you to tell me about yourself. Start as far back as you can remember and tell me your life story." Joshua took two very deep and intensional breaths then added oil to Gweneth's feet, calves, and legs, up to where the towel was covering.
He started with Gweneth's left foot and began to work her lower body with smooth delicate strokes and listened while Gweneth

started to tell him about growing up in south Florida.

• • • •

Sixty-three minutes had passed and Gweneth was now laying on her back with her arms by her sides and her legs together, toes pointing upwards. From across the room, she appeared as still as a cadaver. Gweneth was very much alive and her nervous system was in a state of perpetual bliss. It was like being paralyzed by the peak intensity of an average orgasm for ten minutes straight. During that time Gweneth was consciously in a self-induced dream state as the human brain blocks intense pain and pleasure from the conscious mind.

Joshua was sitting in a chair just a few feet from the bed, waiting for Gweneth to wake up. His eyes were closed and the way his chest was moving in and out would make one believe he was sleeping. However he was fully conscious and he certainly wasn't asleep, at least not yet. He was breathing and meditating while Gweneth was on her first of three personal journeys, connecting her consciousness with her sexual and spiritual energies. Joshua was building and storing potential energy so he would be prepared when Gweneth awoke, fully conscious.

If the first part of the ritual was successful Gweneth would remember everything that had transpired the previous day including her meeting with Susan and meeting Joshua two different times before gaining access to his hotel room. She would remember Joshua's massage and as the massage progressed, she started weeping, then laughing.

When Joshua started massaging areas between Gweneth's legs, she worked through feelings and emotions she had suppressed many years prior. With one of Joshua's hands over Gweneth's vulva and the other on Gweneth's heart, after several minutes, she felt any suppressed pain, shame, embarrassment, and blocks, disappear and opened herself up to unfiltered and pure sexual energy. Such a rush of pleasure can cause one to hallucinate and experience an out-of-body dream state.

Joshua did not know what Gweneth had blocked and suppressed from her past or what her reaction would be when waking up. He did know, from past experiences, that after awakening from such a powerful surge of sexual energy most women have a strong and primal urge to mate. Even if the woman prefers clitoral stimulation her sex drive is craving the hardness of a man inside her.
This surge can last an hour or two and then both man and woman drift off and sleep together for several more hours before a similar ritual starts again. Occasionally, something goes wrong. If Gweneth were to wake up and not remember anything from the past twenty-four hours, she might have already failed her training. If she were to wake up and still believe she's the woman who was in Joshua's room waiting for him, the ritual would have to be completed again and with a much lower chance of success.
Either of those scenarios would mean that Joshua failed his test and, as a result, Gweneth would fail hers.

Joshua opened his eyes and quietly stood up. He had to use the bathroom and did not want to turn on the light or make any more noise than necessary. He slowly closed the bathroom door and sat down on the toilet to pee.
Joshua quietly washed his hands and face after flushing the toilet. He opened the door and quietly walked out of the bathroom to find Gweneth sitting up and breathing in rhythm. She looked at Joshua and smiled.

"What the fuck was that?" She asked, obviously happy to see him.

"That ritual was the first of three phases we are going to complete over the next twenty-four hours." Joshua explained. "How much do you remember?"

"I remember everything." Gweneth said, still smiling. "I remember the guy at the grocery store. I remember driving to South Beach, my meeting with Susan, meeting you in the conference room, and talking with you after your presentation."

Gweneth stopped and took an extra breath, then continued. "I remember coming into your room, almost leaving- feeling rejected and then…" Gweneth stopped again.

"And then what?" Joshua asked.

"And then…almost literally reborn. I can remember things from my past and have memories I had completely forgotten. Good memories." Gweneth explained.

"Any not-so-good memories?" Joshua asked.

"Maybe a few, but they're foggy and don't have any weight to them. At least not anymore." Gweneth stood up and stretched her arms over her head and twisted at the waist. "I have to use the bathroom." She said walking towards Joshua. She stopped in front of him and looked at his face and connected with his eyes. Gweneth put her head on his chest and wrapped her arms around him.

"Thank you. For whatever you did, thank you." Gweneth said. She felt stronger and more alive and had the urge to take Joshua right there. Her urge to pee was more immediate and took precedence. "I'm sorry. I really do have to use the bathroom." Gweneth quickly untangled herself from Joshua and walked into the bathroom, closing the door halfway.

When she was finished, Gweneth washed her hands and face and used a warm washcloth on her body. As she was wiping herself down she noticed how wet she was and it wasn't from peeing. Gweneth inserted two fingers into herself which was enough to trigger an intense rush of pleasure that induced a flood of hormones. Gweneth recognized her instincts and started taking slow deep breaths.

"Joshua?" She asked. "You've done this ritual before, right?"

"Yes, several times, however not recently."

"So, if I were to tell you that I think I might be the most turned-on I've ever been in my life, is that normal?"

"You should come out here and ask me that." Joshua suggested.

Gweneth walked out of the bathroom still holding the washcloth. She didn't see Joshua standing where he was for their embrace. Instead, he was laying on the bed, fully erect and breathing very quickly.

"Oh my God." Gweneth said. "I guess this isn't unexpected then." She tossed the washcloth back into the bathroom, walked over to the side of the bed, and gave Joshua a very slow sensual kiss. She ran her hands through his hair then down his neck and shoulders. The smell of Joshua's pheromones and the taste of his breath were like pouring gasoline on an already massive bonfire.

As Gweneth was about to mount Joshua she realized the music had stopped and her hair was also down and unbrushed. Gweneth stood up and retrieved her hair tie from the nightstand and within seconds she had her hair in a ponytail. Gweneth changed CDs and turned the volume on the speakers up just enough to question whether it was too loud for four-thirty in the morning.
She crawled up from the foot of the bed and stopped when she reached Joshua's waist.
Her hands were wrapped around his body as she kissed his thighs and below his stomach. Each kiss started with the tip of her tongue and ended with the release of her lips and a cool exhale of breath through her nose.

Joshua's member grew even harder before Gweneth's eyes and the pulse of power gave Gweneth the same flood of hormones she felt in the bathroom, her fingers barely penetrating but swimming in sexual energy.

Without hesitation, Gweneth took a deep breath in through her nose and locked eyes with Joshua. Their breathing had started to synchronize and with direct eye contact, their energies started to weave together. Gweneth started kissing the base and shaft of Joshua's penis as she moved her hands, gripping the side of his butt with her right and using her left hand to gently lift his member so she had access to the royal family. Three sweet kisses for each Prince while her left fingertips danced with the crown of the King.

From the base of the shaft, Gweneth touched the tip of her tongue to every inch Joshua had. She teased the third eye of Joshua's shaft causing another throbbing pulse. Gweneth, very slowly, took Joshua fully into her mouth.

The hardness Gweneth felt sliding in and out of her mouth was accelerating her breathing as she was trying to control her instinct to touch herself. Finally, she slid all of Joshua from her mouth, using her lips to leave behind a thin layer of saliva on the tip.

Gweneth positioned herself on top of Joshua and felt him between her legs. She moved her hips back and forth, then side to side, smothering the King in a bath of sexual essence. Gweneth leaned down, her breasts flattening against Joshua's chest.

She kissed him deeply and passionately for as long as she could before breaking the kiss and locking eyes just seconds before Gweneth slid Joshua inside her.

Gweneth made love to Joshua for almost two hours. They moved slowly with intention and grace, weaving their energies together in a cocoon of sensual bliss. They both maintained deep and rhythmic breathing, sharing the element of life through the bridge of tongues and lips.

As Gweneth was moments from climax Joshua would slowly put himself all the way inside of her and stop, resting his strength inside such a powerful and warm blanket. Her energy building, transferring from member to mate.

After several peaks and no valleys, Joshua let Gweneth erupt like a fountain of youthful, untamed energy. She came for what seemed like minutes, and the afterglow lasted far longer. Both charged and exhausted, it was time to let their bodies recover.

Before they fell asleep in each other's arms, Gweneth and Joshua shared a shower and took turns bathing each other. It was very sensual however the intention was not arousal, but gratitude and purity. The shower was not a normal part of the ritual but fit within the same ideals and purpose.

Non-verbal communication had taken place between them since Gweneth had first taken Joshua deep in her mouth. Their energies had come together so perfectly, their communication was beyond what words could describe. It was emotional communication through conduits that cannot be seen or heard, only felt. Gweneth's thoughts and emotions were shared and realized by Joshua as the two became closer to one, even if for a short time.

After the shower ended and toweling each other dry, they laid on the bed, staring into each other's eyes. The moment Gweneth closed hers was the sign Joshua could close his. Gweneth dreamed of freedom and soaring through clouds. Gliding over mountain ridges and using warm thermals to rise high above the earth, seeing for miles in every direction.

Joshua did not dream for the five hours they slept. He rested peacefully knowing Gweneth was now free from her own imposed blocks and limitations. They still had a lot of work to do, but Joshua knew Gweneth would pass without question. They fell asleep, embraced chest to chest and awoke in the same position just before noon.

With Gweneth still asleep, Joshua opened his eyes and remembered all the events from the night before, including being drugged and programmed in the elevator, minutes before meeting Gweneth.

CHAPTER 2

Monday, November 11th
3:13 pm

Gweneth parked her car at the Ritz-Carlton South Beach and checked her makeup and hair in the mirror behind the lowered sun-shade. After a mist of body spray, she felt confident and ready for an interview she hoped would be a big stepping stone in her young career.

Gweneth turned twenty-one a few months earlier and was enjoying her freedom, now legally an adult. Gweneth had been working at a call center for the past two years while finishing her Associate's Degree in marketing at a local community college. She was ambitious and wanted more. Gweneth was very responsible with money and saved most of her income. She worked on different projects at the call center and moved up, into the ranks of the training department, but she felt she was not earning close to what her potential was.

Gweneth applied for an entry-level position with a marketing firm that paid more than the call center and offered her the opportunity to network and gain experience in a field she felt passionate about. Gweneth dreamed of a career as an executive for a marketing firm or working for a Fortune 500 company.

Before college, Gweneth was a member of a championship-winning cheerleading squad, which spent almost as much time fundraising as they did practicing. Gweneth's personality and enthusiasm shined during fundraisers as she had a way of making a normally awkward situation comfortable by explaining the "why" behind the donation request. People often gave more than requested because Gweneth made them feel as if it was an investment rather than charity.

Gweneth walked into the hotel lobby holding a small organizer in one hand and her car keys in another. She wore a navy blue pants suit she bought specifically for this interview. Her call center wardrobe consisted of faded denim and hoodies. Gweneth followed signs directing her to a conference room with a sign that read: **Redhawk Marketing.**
As she reached for the door handle a young woman called Gweneth's name. "Gwen Cooper?"

Gweneth turned and looked at the beautiful woman walking toward her, hand extended and smiling.
"Yes. That's me. Are you Susan?" Gweneth accepted her invitation and shook her hand. Her grip was stronger than Gweneth anticipated.

"No, I'm not Susan. I'm Susan's assistant Trish Blackman. Nice to meet you."

Gweneth felt slightly embarrassed and intimidated. She knew Susan Patterson's voice from a phone interview a few days prior and Trish's voice was distinctly different. Gweneth thought Trish was in her late twenties. Her slim figure accentuated perfect posture and confidence she imposed effortlessly. Gweneth also identified a slight Japanese accent that matched a mysteriously attractive Asian ancestry.

"Trish nice to meet you." Gweneth said with a sincere smile.

"Any problems finding the hotel?" Trish asked.

"Not at all. I've been here before, or to the beachside of the hotel anyway." Gweneth was still smiling. "Are we meeting in here?" She asked, reaching again for the handle on the conference room door.

Trish stopped her quickly. "No, actually Susan would like to meet with you privately, in a separate office." Trish carefully put her arm out and turned Gweneth away from the conference room doors, casually touching Gweneth's right shoulder.
Gweneth gave the slightest smile and felt confident she was going to land the job. She followed Trish to a bank of elevators to the west of the lobby.

As they approached the second elevator, it opened without either of them pressing the call button. A young woman stepped off the elevator without making eye contact with either Gweneth or Trish and was walking in a very assertive but broken posture. It was obvious she had recently been crying.
Gweneth took a deep breath as if she was going to say something to the random person passing her but she couldn't find the right word, context or situation to ask if she was ok. Trish acted as if the young woman getting off the elevator wasn't even there and passed her at the same point, walking through the elevator doors.

Trish pushed the button for the sixth floor and the elevator doors closed.
"Susan tells me you're interested in photography?" Trish asked before the elevator started moving.

"Oh, just as a hobby." Replied Gweneth. "I'm not very good yet."

"How did you become interested?" Trish asked while reaching for Gweneth's right shoulder once more. She grabbed a single stray hair from Gweneth's collar and held it out for Gweneth to see. She dropped the hair and let it fall weightlessly.

Gweneth answered as she watched the hair slowly fall to the elevator floor.
"I had to take an art class for my degree and I chose photography. It was fun, so I've kept taking pictures and it's something I do to

escape."

Gweneth felt herself talking too much and tried to save the conversation with a question. "Do you enjoy photography?"

"I do. I just bought a new camera and the first few pictures I took came out quite well."
Trish stopped talking as the elevator doors opened and standing there was a mature and very attractive woman, standing 5'10" without heels. She had a toned body and a long frame which she covered with an expensive business suit. She wore a modest amount of makeup and jewelry that accented a perfect smile.

"Gwen. I'm Susan Patterson. It's nice to meet you."

Gweneth was a bit stunned. Instincts took over and she introduced herself. "Nice to meet you Susan." Gweneth said while extending a hand toward her as she stepped off the elevator. Trish stayed standing in the exact same spot and didn't move.

"Thank you Trish." Susan said, very cavalier.

Trish smiled and nodded. "Nice to meet you, Gwen."

"Nice to meet you too." Gweneth replied, just as the elevator doors were closing.

Susan shook Gweneth's hand with both of hers then put her arm around her as they started to walk down the hall.

"How do you put up with this humidity?" Susan asked, giving Gweneth's shoulder a slight squeeze. "I'm from Arizona where it's hot and dry."
After several steps, Susan let go of Gweneth's shoulder and returned her arms to her sides.

"I guess I've lived here so long it's become normal." Gweneth was walking a bit faster to keep up with Susan's long strides.
They quickly reached room 6015 and Susan opened the door with an electronic key card, a new addition to the hotel. Gweneth felt

strange. She'd been to several job interviews but never one in a hotel room. Walking in, Gweneth discovered it was not a typical hotel room. It was a one-bedroom suite that had been rearranged to make it a two-room office. Instead of a bed, there was a workstation and a small kitchenette in the main room. A few steps away the bedroom had a larger desk with a laptop computer and a few post-it notes, scattered in various positions. There were two chairs facing the desk which also had a small shaded lamp and a hotel phone in the corner.

"Gweneth, please have a seat." Susan said, directing her to a chair in front of the desk. "Would you like a bottled water?" Susan reached into a small refrigerator next to the desk and pulled out a bottled water for herself.

"Thank you. That would be great." Gweneth answered.

Susan handed Gweneth the first bottle then reached for another and started to ask a question as Gweneth took a long sip of water.

"Are you a spiritual person Gweneth?"

Gweneth was caught off guard. "Ah, yes." She paused. "I would consider myself spiritual, but not religious."

"Why is that?" Susan challenged Gweneth to elaborate.

Gweneth wanted to ask what this had to do with the job interview, however, she also felt compelled to answer the question.
"Every religion believes their way is the right way, and in many cases the only way, and all other belief systems are wrong. I do believe that there is a life force - or God, or Power greater than ourselves, but I don't think we are actually capable of understanding this higher power."

Gweneth was surprised how freely she shared her own spiritual philosophy with someone so quickly and started to ask, "What..."

Susan interrupted immediately.
"I know you're wondering why I'm asking you these questions,

and I have an answer for you." Susan, receiving unblinking eye contact with Gweneth. "You are interviewing for a position at Redhawk Marketing. I am a specialized recruiter for a unique program we have. We only extend ten invitations to our training program each year. Typically, only half of the candidates finish the program and become field managers."

Susan paused and broke eye contact with Gweneth, who then blinked several times. She felt different but couldn't put her finger on how. Her mind was racing with questions and she had a difficult time narrowing down which one to ask first. Susan was watching Gweneth process what she'd explained to her so far.

"Gwen." Susan said. Gweneth looked straight up and made eye contact with Susan once again. "The reason you're having a difficult time focusing is that you are under a very mild induced hypnosis. I'm going to teach you how to reverse it or return to your fully present and conscious self."
Susan sat up straight in her chair.
"Sit up straight and take a deep breath. When you exhale, I want you to sigh as naturally and fully as you can."

Gweneth took a deep breath in through her nose and out through her mouth with a mild sigh and was still making eye contact with Susan as she followed her instructions.

"Gwen, you can do better than that." Susan continued. "We're going to try again, and this time take a deep breath into the pit of your stomach, as far down as it will go. Then close your eyes and hold that breath."

Susan completed the request as well and Gweneth followed along. "As you exhale, think of all your fears, worries and stress, rushing out of your body with your breath. I want to hear a sigh that releases all of it. Let it go, out into the universe."

With her eyes closed, Gweneth took a few seconds and exhaled a much more powerful sigh. At the end of her breath she smiled with true relief.

"Much better. Now, open your eyes and follow this pattern of breathing." Susan again, demonstrated as she explained.
"Take a breath in through your nose. Visualize that breath traveling deep into your lungs and continuing to the pit of your stomach. Then imagine the air traveling back up, through your body, and exhale for eight seconds. Then repeat the same breath again."

Gweneth took five long breaths as Susan sat back in her chair and gave Gweneth a look of approval. "How do you feel?" Susan asked.

"Good." Gweneth said. She looked around the room and then back at Susan.

"You said I was under hypnosis, although I don't remember being hypnotized or consenting to be hypnotized."

"The test is to see if you can be induced without knowing." Susan started to explain. "The reason we do this test is that there are different types of people and some are not capable of being induced. More importantly, they're not capable of recognizing or reversing it. You passed all three phases wonderfully." Susan smiled and sat forward in her chair.

Gweneth tried to force a smile but was still not sure what all of this was about.

"The first level of hypnosis is suggestion. Trish, my assistant, put your mind in a suggestive state once you got into the elevator. I completed the process as we walked down the hall. This is not a trick or illusion and this is why we are as selective as we are."

Gweneth sat slightly forward, but her expression didn't change as she took another long sip of water.

"Once we sat down you could feel that something was off. You felt compelled to answer my questions, but could sense they weren't the right questions. You were then able to complete a remedial breathing exercise on your first attempt to return to your fully conscious self. Well done Gwen."

"Thanks. But I'm still not sure what hypnosis and breathing has to do with marketing? Or if it's legal?" Gweneth asked.

"I can tell you that we are not a direct marketing company, and most companies have never heard of us or what we do. I can't tell you anymore until you've signed a non-disclosure agreement and agree to enter our training program, but I can give you an idea of compensation."

Gweneth was silent as Susan slid an unsealed envelope across the desk.

"If you complete the training and start taking on your own clients, this would be your starting salary for the first year."

Gweneth opened the envelope and pulled out a small card with only a dollar amount printed on it.

$200,000

Gweneth's eyes opened wide and her mouth dropped slightly before she caught herself.

"This is a lot more than I was expecting." Gweneth was currently making $8.00 per hour at the call center which was $2.00 above minimum wage. She was hoping to start a new position at $10.00 per hour which would be almost $21,000 a year.
"Are you sure you have the right person?" Gweneth asked. "I'm not sure I'm qualified for an executive position."

Susan smiled and a small chuckle escaped as Gweneth finished her statement. "Gweneth Cooper." Susan said, using her full name for the first time. "You are absolutely the right person, and don't worry, it's not an executive position the way you are thinking of it. You would be starting at the bottom and will have to prove yourself through training and as an account manager to start moving up the ladder. We only employ twelve account account managers, all of whom you will be competing with to start your job as they will be competing with you to keep theirs."

Susan stopped talking and watched as Gweneth processed everything, trying to make a decision. She finished her bottled water then asked, "If I turn down this offer, is there consideration outside this program?"

"That's a good question Gwen." Susan sat forward and leaned slightly over the desk. "I'm going to share something with you that I've never shared with any other candidate at this point." Susan looked Gweneth directly in the eyes. "If you decline this opportunity, there's nothing else we can offer you."
Susan's tone changed and she spoke very carefully.
"If you decline, I am obligated to assist you in forgetting this meeting transpired the way it did. I would give you a similar but false memory of you not getting the job you applied for, and you'd leave and return to your life as you knew it thirty minutes ago."
Gweneth thought of the young woman who got off the elevator, crying, and obviously upset. Trish's coldness to her reinforced Gweneth's intuition that she must have said no.
Susan sat back in her chair. "Or, you can join our company, work hard learning skills that will give you opportunities that an extremely low number of people have. Our top account managers are earning seven figures a year and they're only in their mid and late 20's. I've had one woman stay past the age of thirty."

"Why does everyone leave before they're thirty?" Gweneth asked.

"They retire." Susan stated. "I've already shared more with you than anybody I have ever interviewed." Susan took a deep breath in through her nose and slowly exhaled through her mouth, hardly noticeable.
"I'll need an answer soon. You can't leave the room and you can't call anyone to help you with the decision. This is entirely on you."

Gweneth sat back in her chair and quickly did a mental pros and cons list. She even considered the fact that she could still be under some type of hypnosis. She did the same breathing routine she had done moments before but more subdued and less obvious. After several breaths, Gweneth was convinced that she was of sound mind and body.

She thought of her mother and sister and how that kind of salary could go a long way to helping those closest to her. She made a decision, but had one important question.
"Susan, I'm completely blown away. I'm almost in shock, but not in shock. I know you've shared more with me than you're comfortable with, but I do have one important question."

Susan was intrigued. "What's your one question?"

"Your job isn't to recruit assassins, is it?" Gweneth asked with a seriousness which Susan thought was a bit dark and a bit comical.

"No." Susan stated with the same seriousness as Gweneth's question. Then a smile emerged. "We are not assassins."

Gweneth smiled. "Then I accept your offer to…" She paused. "Whatever this is."
Susan returned the smile and handed Gweneth a document.
"This is your Non-Disclosure Agreement. Take as much time as you need, and read everything, twice. I can't persuade you to sign, you have to do that on your own."
Susan then handed Gweneth a larger document, this one had a binder clip instead of a paper clip.
"This is your contract." Susan smiled. "Same rules apply. Feel free to use the desk out there." Susan motioned to the workstation in the main room.
"I'm going to the cafe in the lobby. They have the best Chai-Tea Latte I've ever had. Would you like anything?"

"I love Chai-Tea." Gweneth replied. "If you don't mind, I'd love one."

"That's why I asked." Susan said. "I'll be back in fifteen minutes or so. Oh, two things I forgot to tell you. If you have plans tonight you should cancel them. Don't go into any details as to why, but your training starts tonight."

Gweneth realized she did have plans with friends, but knew she could reschedule. "Ok, but should I put in my two weeks notice with…"

Susan interrupted. "Read your NDA, and your Contract. There's an envelope in front of the last page. Open it only after you sign your contract. It's your first paycheck."
Susan smiled and left the hotel room leaving Gweneth alone with a good amount of reading to do. Gweneth sat down in an uncomfortable ergonomic chair and started reading her NDA. It was three pages of what she could disclose and what was proprietary information about a job she knew nothing about. The language was vague in areas, and more specific when more legal terms were used.

After reading the NDA twice Gweneth felt she comprehended what she read. It was difficult to associate what was being described as Gweneth still did not understand what her job was. She decided to read the contract before signing anything.

The contract read, as Gweneth imagined, like an employment contract for an Account Manager at a successful marketing firm. She then remembered that Susan said she would change her memory if she declined. 'Why wasn't that my first question?' Gweneth thought to herself.

She finished reading the contract for the second time and realized it had been forty minutes since Susan had left the hotel room. Gweneth stood up from the desk and stretched her arms out. She started walking around the small room, thinking about everything she'd read and why she hadn't signed yet. She didn't have any other questions for Susan except, "What the fuck is this?"

After waiting a few more minutes for Susan to return, Gweneth sat down at the small desk and picked up the pen next to the phone. She signed her name where indicated and did the same for the contract, completing several pages needing initials and a few checked boxes. Gweneth then opened the envelope that Susan mentioned containing her first paycheck. As she pulled the check from the envelope Gweneth's eyes grew incredibly wide.

The check was made out to Gweneth Cooper in the amount of $20,000. Gweneth had never possessed or seen that amount of money in her lifetime.

Gweneth grew up in a modest, middle-class home where there was always food on the table and a few small gifts for Christmas, but nothing extravagant or luxurious and certainly not checks for $20,000.

Gweneth was proud she had saved $2300 over the past year which was double the $1100 she saved the year prior. After two years of working countless hours at a call center with terrible coffee, Gweneth thought, 'whatever this job is, I'm going to do it, even if it is to be an assassin.'

Gweneth was still looking at the check when the door opened and Susan returned with two cups of Chai-Tea. It had only been two minutes since Gweneth signed the NDA and contract. She immediately knew the timing wasn't a coincidence.

Susan spoke first, confirming Gweneth's intuition.

"It took you longer than normal." She handed Gweneth's Chai-Tea to her and picked up the signed documents. "It might be on the cold side."

Susan continued. "Almost everyone signs within the first ten minutes. Some sign as soon as they see the amount of the check which is the first thing they look at."

"You said not to open the envelope until after I signed." Gweneth recalled, almost defending herself.

"You followed my instructions perfectly." Susan walked into her micro-office and sat down behind her desk. "Come have a seat." Susan said just before taking a sip of her Chai.

"I'm curious." Gweneth stated. "You were in a neighboring room, or across the hall perhaps? Watching?" Gweneth sat down in front of Susan.

"Yes." Susan stated. "What was I watching?"

"You were watching me, waiting for me to sign those." Gweneth stated obviously. "You were also watching to see if I followed your instructions, as you pointed out."

"All of those are easy answers. What else was I watching?" Susan asked.

Gweneth thought for a moment. "My reaction to the check."

"Very impressive. Why?" Susan challenged.

"There could be a number of reasons, but I'll bet most people just don't stare at it." Gweneth replied.

"Would it surprise you that there has only been one other person to take longer to sign than you did?"

"No, that doesn't surprise me. Even if you told me it was two million dollars in that envelope I still would have done the best I could to make sure I understood as much as possible and that everything was legal and ethical." Gweneth found herself breathing in rhythm again, not consciously.

"The NDA and Contract." Susan sat forward in her chair. "They are tests but the NDA is quite real." Susan inserted Gweneth's signed NDA into a folder on her desk then picked up the contract and looked at three different pages.
"The contract is a different story. How much of it did you understand or comprehend?" Susan asked.

"I understood about seventy-five percent and comprehended about ninety percent of that." Gweneth spoke with more candor now. She felt comfortable and more at ease. "Susan, what is this business?" Gweneth asked.

Susan's focus shifted from Gweneth to her signature on the contract then back at the young, naive, and talented woman sitting across from her. "This contract has nothing to do with our business here." Susan said, ripping the contract in half, then in half again and tossed it in a waste basket next to the desk.

Gweneth sat up quickly. "I don't understand. The contract was just a test?"

"It seems you understand perfectly. The contract was a few different tests. You initialed page six and eight. You voluntarily answered the two questions on page five, and you followed all the instructions perfectly." Susan smiled again. "You're one of our best recruits. Ever."

"Recruits for what?" Gweneth asked again, with more seriousness.

"We are a firm that specializes in influence." Susan started to explain. "If you are a CEO and want to influence a board member to vote a certain way without threatening, blackmail or bribery, you would call us. If you want to plant an idea in someone's head, or erase an idea from someone's head, you would call us.
We use several different types of conscious and subconscious influence and combine them with the most powerful and raw energy in the body. Sexual energy."

"I'm not sure I'm following you." Gweneth took a breath and continued. "You are hired to change people's minds using hypnosis and sexual energy?"

Susan smiled. "We incorporate hypnosis and we use a technology called NLP or Neuro-linguistic Programming. It's a different way of communicating with someone's nervous system to produce a desired response." Susan stopped and took another sip of her Chai-Tea.

"When you break down a basic idea or behavior, you can literally program the human brain like a computer. Basic ideas and behaviors don't require a lot of programming, and little maintenance. Larger ideas, or the more delicate the mind, the more complicated things can get."

"What do you mean when you say sexual energy?" Gweneth asked.

"Sexual energy is the most potent and abundant energy in the body. If directed in the right ways, it can help solidify any type of influence to behavior, thought, or neurological response you want. If you are going to write a program for a mechanical computer you write code. The biological computer that is our brain doesn't operate on 1's and 0's. It can't be programmed by a machine. We use touch, emotion, neurology, physcology, and some forms of hypnosis to create a "program" for the human brain."

"This doesn't sound like the most legal business." Gweneth stated.

"It's not. We are very much like the CIA, except we are not government funded and we don't get immunity if we get caught." Susan sat forward in her chair and decided to start a new line of questioning. "How do you feel about sex Gwen?"

"How do I feel about it?" Gweneth repeated the question. "I think I feel as most people do. Sex is great."

"How many partners have you had in your lifetime?"

"This is getting kind of personal. I'm not sure I want to share this kind of stuff."

"Interesting." Susan said.

"Why is that interesting?" Gweneth asked.

"All indications show that you are quite open sexually. But you feel uncomfortable talking about sex?" Susan asked, more curious than concerned.

"I consider myself open minded, but I don't really talk about my sex life with anybody, even my boyfriend."

"Yes, Scott. How often do the two of you make love?"

"Ah,...We've only been dating a few months. I would say one or two times a week." Gweneth shifted in her chair.

"Only once or twice a week?" Susan confirming. "It must not be that good of sex."

Gweneth took a little offense to Susan's assumption, however she was right. "We're still getting to know each other." Gweneth said.

"I see. Now my questions will get more personal and sexual. Honesty is the biggest factor. Not for my benefit, but for your own. It's sometimes easier if you're more relaxed. Would you like to relax a little more?"

Gweneth was slightly confused. "Relax how?"

"When you arrived, Trish and I combined two very simple NLP and hypnosis exercises to put you in a specific state of wanting to tell the truth. You identified that state pretty quickly and I showed you how to return to your fully conscious self."
Susan continued. "You can induce different states in your own conscious mind much easier than I can. If you want to be 100% honest with yourself, there's a recipe for that. If you want to hide the truth or a truth, there's a recipe for that. If you know what recipe you want for a specific state or outcome, with practice, you can recall or access different states very quickly."

Gweneth took in everything Susan had explained, closed her eyes and started the only breathing technique she knew. Susan sat silently and let Gweneth breathe without interruption. It had been just under a minute when Gweneth spoke.

"I'm ready." She said, then continued. "Ask me anything."

Susan sat forward in her chair, almost in disbelief. "Are you sure you're ready?"

"Yes. Ask me anything? " Gweneth opened her eyes and made contact with Susans.

Susan didn't hesitate. "What is your full name?"

"Gweneth Ashley Cooper." Gweneth gave Susan a sarcastic smile.

"Why did you sign the contract?" Susan asked, taking the final sip of her Chai-Tea.

Gweneth took a conscious deep breath in between her more rhythmic breathing. "The money."

"When was the last time you pleased yourself sexually?"

Gweneth didn't hesitate with her answer. "This morning."

"Who or what were you thinking about while you were touching yourself?"

Gweneth smiled at the thought of her fantasy and after a short pause answered the question. "My neighbor Brian."

"Why didn't you fantasize about Scott?"

"Scott is a nice guy, but he's not aggressive enough. He is very sensual but he lacks a degree of masculinity." Gweneth held her posture perfectly and continued breathing in rhythm however it was becoming less noticeable.

"Have you ever imagined being with another woman while you pleasure yourself?" Susan asked.

"I have, but rarely." Gweneth responded with no further explanation.

"Are you attracted to women?" Susan was more specific.

"Instinctually, no." Gweneth continued. "There have been two friends that I've become attracted to over time but I've always preferred the company of men."

Susan sat back in her chair. "How many sexual partners have you had?"

"Four men, two women." Gweneth answered.

"I'm going to ask the next several questions quickly. No long explanations needed, just short answers." Susan eluded. "Have you ever engaged in a threesome or group sex?"

"No."

"Have you engaged in anal sex?"

"Yes. Once."

"Did you enjoy it?"

"No."

"How many sexual releases do you have a day?"

"On average - one."

"How old were you when you had sex for the first time?"

"Sixteen."

"How old were you when you made love for the first time?"

"Nineteen."

"Was the difference distinguishable?"

"Absolutely."

"Do you enjoy giving oral sex to men?"

"Yes."

"Do you enjoy receiving oral sex from men or women?"

"Women more than men, and yes I enjoy it."

"How many times a day do you fantasize about any type of sexual contact?"

"At least once a minute."

"Would you ever have sex for money?"

Gweneth didn't answer right away. She thought about the question. Up until that point, she had never asked herself that question before.

She tried to maintain her posture and breathing, but it was interrupted when Gweneth asked a question in response. "Is that what this is?"
Susan didn't move a muscle. "You didn't answer the question." Susan repeated it. "Would you have sex for money?"

"No." Gweneth answered.

"Think about the question." Susan said. "The question doesn't specify how much money, or who the sex would be with. What if the man was good looking, confident and funny, and the money was one million dollars, for one or two nights together? Would you turn down one million dollars?

"No, I wouldn't." Gweneth responded confidently.

"So I'll ask the previous question again. Would you have sex for money?"

"No, I wouldn't have sex for money. I would spend time with someone as a travel companion or confidant, but that's between two consenting adults and has nothing to do with money."

Susan sat up in her chair. "I understand why you answered the way you did and that's fine, but this isn't a legal question, or a morality question." Susan paused and thought for a moment. She looked at Gweneth and asked, "Would you consent to sex with Trish, tonight, for $100,000?"

Gweneth was stunned. "Seriously?"

Susan looked Gweneth square in the eyes. "Seriously."

Gweneth looked away and down towards the floor. Her breathing pattern had completely changed, lacking rhythm and awareness. Her breath was shallow and the pace had picked up. She was starting to panic just enough that Susan decided to explain, but Gweneth answered, both women speaking at the same time.

"Yes." Gweneth said.

"It's just a test." Susan stated. "Pay attention to how you're breathing now. That whole line of questioning was to see what made you uncomfortable enough to break your breathing pattern. The point of the last question was to show that everyone has a price. The majority of people won't admit to having a price, but everyone does. It's not always about sex or money, but in most instances, one or the other will typically prevail." Susan paused and focused on Gweneth's body language.
"We pose as many different companies that offer a range of different services, but for what we are best at, most of our work is done through a referral only based escort service." Susan answered.
"The processes we use in influencing some of the most powerful people in the world utilizes sexual energy because of it's anchor to our subconscious." Susan paused again to gauge Gweneth's reaction which was more inquisitive.

Susan continued. "Sexual energy can be used for healing physical and psychological illness. It can be used to promote fertility for obvious reasons, as well as contribute to a healthy immune system and prolong youthfulness as we age. If you combine sexual energy with NLP, hypnosis, subliminal messaging, direct suggestion, or at the very least a Quid pro qo, the success rate of your desired outcome is over ninety-three percent."

Gweneth began to understand what she had signed up for. She

relaxed in her chair, and closed her eyes again, focusing only on her breath. She spoke, still with her eyes shut.

"How many clients does a typical account manager handle?"

"It depends on our workload and what is required for a specific client, but on average, two accounts at a time with meetings once or twice a month, per account."

"As an account manager, do we sleep with our clients to program them?"

"Not necessarily. Sometimes no physical contact is necessary. Other instances have required several sessions of programming. Not all programming requires sex or physical touch. Sexual and sensual energy can be manifested in different ways."

"Are there any more big surprises I should be prepared for?" Gweneth asked.

"Too many to list." Susan answered with a smile. "Are you ready to start your training?"

Gweneth took a deep breath and thought about that very moment in her life. This was something that was completely unexpected, unimagined, and not something Gweneth had any experience in. Sexual energy, hypnosis, powerful people, all areas she had little knowledge of.

She summed up her only hesitation in two words. "Why me?"

"We do extensive research on candidates before we contact them, including an interaction they are completely unaware of. We use this interaction as a way to measure one's potential energy, and yours is off the chart. We spoke on the phone the next day as a formality. The rest you know." Susan confided in Gweneth like an older sister explaining the ways of life to a younger sibling.

"I tested off the chart in potential energy?" Gweneth asked as if she was reading some type of quantum physics equation. "When was this interaction?"

"The day before we spoke on the phone you stopped by the grocery store on your way home from work. While in line you engaged in conversation with the gentleman behind you. He flirted with you. Do you remember?" Susan asked.

"I do remember him. He was nice. He was a little older so I didn't take his flirting seriously."

"But you did flirt back. Maybe not consciously, however your energy changed quickly by his measurement, and that's when you became someone I became very interested in meeting."
Susan shifted in her chair. "Remember when I said some people aren't capable of being induced, or aren't capable of recognizing it? That's because their energy isn't as compatible with others. Your energy is compatible with almost anyones, and that is very rare." Susan explained.

"Now, are you ready to start your training?"

Gweneth took one more deep breath and then committed using only two words.
"I'm ready."

CHAPTER 3

Tuesday, 11:43am

After separate stints of time in the bathroom both Gweneth and Joshua decided room service would be best. Joshua was keeping a low profile and didn't want to be seen in the hotel, not conducting his workshop on NLP.

After they both shared various forms of protein and an impressive fruit bowl, Joshua refocused his attention on Gweneth.

"Are you ready for the next phase of your training?" Joshua asked.

"If it's anything like the last phase, then yes." Gweneth replied, shooting Joshua a wink.

"Actually, the next phase is a little more subdued, but much more important." Joshua stood up and cleared their dishes, setting the tray out in the hallway. He returned to where they had been sitting at a small countertop separating the kitchen from the rest of the room.

"Today, we're going to try to access your spiritual consciousness and if we're successful, you'll have a conversation with God."
"Excuse me?" Gweneth asked, not sure she heard him correctly.

Joshua smiled. "I just wanted to see your reaction when I said that." He stood up and encouraged Gweneth to follow him to the balcony. Joshua pulled the blackout curtains all the way back along with the standard decorative linen.

The beautiful mid day view of South Beach and the Atlantic Ocean was breathtaking. Joshua opened the door and stepped out in the moist Florida air where it was clear and 78 degrees. There was high humidity and the forecast called for thunderstorms later into the afternoon and evening.

"I'm not suggesting you're going to talk to God as most people would think of God." He continued. "I'm going to help you contact your inner Goddess and bring her into your consciousness." Joshua paused.

"It's up to you, and her if and how you communicate."

He paused again, and took Gweneth's hand. There was an immediate transfer of energy between both of them. Although small, it was enough for both of them to feel it.

"Most people don't realize how small and connected we all are. Look out at the ocean and the people on the beach. You can see how insignificantly small each of us is when compared to the world around us."

Joshua turned and faced Gweneth. "The energy inside us connects with the energies of the world every day. There is so much we can't see with our eyes, but we can use other senses to interact with almost anything imaginable. The most basic instincts we have are hardwired into our DNA. Our need to procreate or mate is not only our strongest primal instinct, it's the easiest to act on since we are the only mammals who mate for pleasure and try to prevent procreation."

Joshua moved behind Gweneth and spoke softly into her left ear.

"Close your eyes, listen and breathe. Take a deep breath in for five seconds and a quick exhale for three."

Joshua started breathing in the same rhythm. After several breaths Joshua continued.

"I want you to visualize each breath traveling down from your lungs into your womb, and then to the base of your spine. This is where your root chakra lies. When that breath reaches your chakra I want you to visualize it glowing RED like blowing on a hot ember."

Joshua paused and completed several breath cycles before he resumed. Gweneth was focused and trying to visualize what Joshua was describing. Still holding hands, both continued to breathe in tempo.

"Are you visualizing your root chakra?"

"Yes." Gweneth replied softly, almost a whisper.

"What color is it?" Joshua asked.

"Bright RED but glowing almost, orange." Gweneth replied.

"We are going to change our breathing." Joshua eluded as he moved behind Gweneth, placing his hands on her waist. "I want you to breathe in for four seconds and out for four seconds only through your mouth. When the chakra glows bright orange, visualize that color traveling through your womb and into your sex organs." Joshua opening Gweneth's robe and rested his hand above her vulva, the tip of his middle finger resting on the hood of her clit.

"This is where your second chakra lies and it's where all of our sexual energy comes from. Our first chakra connects us to the earth, as we are rooted on land. Our second chakra is where we draw our power from and is also where our inner God or Goddess resides."
Joshua returned his hand to hers and Gweneth could feel her wetness on this tip of his finger.

"Keep this breath going until the orange starts to burn yellow. Then I want you to visualize squeezing my hand, but don't physically squeeze it."

Joshua followed his own instructions and continued breathing with Gweneth. It was only a minute before he felt a very light pulse in his right hand. "Very good. Now open your eyes." Joshua finished.

Gweneth slowly opened her eyes and looked out at the ocean, then up at the sky.
"This is unreal." Gweneth started speaking, but at a slower pace than usual. All the colors around her seemed more vivid and bright. "How did you know I visualized squeezing your hand?"

Joshua smiled. "I'll show you. Close your eyes again, just for a minute. Keep breathing and focus on your left hand."
Joshua made a similar vision in his mind and after only a few seconds Gweneth felt it."

"Oh my God." She said. "How is this possible?"

"It's our nervous systems and conscious minds talking to each other. The focus of your training is to teach you these techniques so that you can induce different states within yourself and others."

"I had no idea this was even possible." Gweneth turned and embraced Joshua, feeling safe and a little overwhelmed.

"We're just getting warmed up. Are you ready to continue inside?" Gweneth took two controlled breaths and released a noticeable sigh. "You're learning." Joshua added.

Gweneth took half a step back and looked up at Joshua. She kissed him softly on the lips then led him back through the patio doors. She sat on the bed as Joshua picked up the hotel phone to call the front desk. He asked for two more pillows and an extra blanket along with two bottles of water.

After hanging up, Gweneth sarcastically teased Joshua. "Whatever you are planning, sounds kinky." She smiled and tossed her hair back, looking at Joshua like he was prey. He recognized the look in her eye and smiled.

"Well, that didn't take long." Joshua said mostly to himself, then to Gweneth. "You should lay back on the bed and open your robe."

She smiled and slid from the foot of the bed to the head in two movements.

"You should come over here and take your robe off." Gweenth said with the same sexy voice she'd used last night when trying to initially seduce Joshua.

"Your Goddess is calling." Joshua said, completely baffling Gweneth.

"What's that?" Were the only words she could form asking as if she didn't hear him correctly.

"Just now, the way you teased me, you're flirting and ready to pounce. Pay attention to how you're breathing." Joshua said slowly and with a slightly deeper voice.

Gweneth noticed her breathing had changed slightly. It was now quicker and shallow.

Joshua continued, "I can tell from your eyes. I would say that it's normal but it's unusual this quickly. We did only a few minutes of breathing and that was enough to let her know you want to make a connection."

"How long does it normally take?" Gweneth asked.

"It can take hours of breathing and focusing energy." Joshua answered.

Gweneth asked, not panicked but firm, "What does that mean?"

"Meditation, relaxation and even some specific sensory adjustments can help increase the chances of a connection. There are many times no true connection is made, even with hours of effort. Your experience early this morning was more powerful than usual and that could also be why she wants to connect. Remember, she's *your* inner Goddess."

"Got it." Gweneth said smiling. She returned to the breathing pattern she had started on the balcony. Joshua could tell from her eyes that she was going to have an interesting journey. He could see a spark, behind her retina, that was eager to escape. He felt the intense desire to kiss her, almost overpowering him. It was another sign that they had to finish what they started and soon. Joshua could not give in to her advances or his own thoughts, even if they weren't one hundred percent his own. He then remembered the first rule. Breathe.

Joshua continued to explain. "It's through neuro-electric channels that we communicate with every cell that make us who we are. There is a point where energy converts from neuro-electric to a spiritual form that we cannot see or measure, only feel. When one can make this conversion a conscious decision, they have attained a level of discipline that is very rare and they can become a very influential person."

Gweneth nodded and a knock on the door shifted Joshua's focus from controlling himself to moving on with Gweneth's journey.

He opened the door and the pillows, blanket and bottled water were sitting outside the door with a small pocket sized envelope resting on top. Joshua picked up the envelope and put it in his robe pocket before bringing the other items into the room.
He set the bottled water on the small counter top and set the pillows and blanket on the bench at the foot of the bed when he noticed Gweneth with her robe open and eyes closed. She was pleasuring herself slowly using the same breathing pattern she had started on the balcony.

Joshua was speechless for several seconds. He was aroused and sat in silence on the foot of the bed and observed Gweneth breathing and navigating her conscious mind, using her clit as a rudder.

Joshua touched Gweneth's left foot with his right hand.
"The mind is more like space than our perceptions of the physical world around us. There isn't a forward or backward, right or left, or even up and down. The only way to effectively navigate one's consciousness is through controlling emotion and thus controlling almost the entire body."

Joshua was concerned Gweneth wasn't aware enough yet to keep the sexual energy of her Goddess contained, however her actions and breathing were dictating otherwise. Joshua continued touching Gweneth's left foot with a warm hand, caressing the top of her toes.

"Gweneth." Joshua said, slowly.

She opened her eyes and continued massaging herself.
"I'm here." She said, gazing deep into Joshua's eyes. He could see she was open, ready, and asking for guidance.

"There are a few things we need to do before we start." Joshua stood up and secured his robe. "For this first part of the ritual, please close your robe around your body, as if it was giving you a hug. Then lay flat on your back with a single pillow under your neck."

Gweneth followed instructions and closed her robe. As she moved into position Joshua cleared the extra pillows from the bed and positioned a single pillow supporting her neck. He retrieved a brown suede blindfold from a bag by the closet and set it on the bed.

"Normally I would ask you to put this on, but I'm going to leave it up to you. It helps with focus, but you seem to have more discipline than most, so it's your choice."

Gweneth put on the blindfold without hesitation. She laid back with her head centered on the pillow and took a deep breath.

"Gweneth. We are going to change our breathing to a slower, deeper and smoother tempo." Joshua spoke slowly and with a deeper voice.
"Take a deep breath in through your nose, into your lungs, then down into your abdomen, just below your stomach. Breathe in slowly until you can't take in any more air. Exhale through your mouth while touching the tip of your tongue to the roof of your

mouth."

Joshua paused while Gweneth took several breaths, finding the correct rhythm. "When you breathe in, use as little effort as possible. When you exhale, let the air fall out of your lungs, don't force it out."

Gweneth made small adjustments as Joshua sat in a chair next to the bed, verbally coaching and keeping tempo with Gweneth. After thirty minutes of conscious breathing he felt ready to play his most important part in Gweneth's journey.

"I'm going to guide you to a decision." Joshua started. "Once we reach our destination, you will choose your own path forward and continue your journey without me. This is an introduction to another part of yourself that will help guide and protect you for the rest of your life."

Gweneth took a deeper breath in, involuntarily, and then resumed her previous technique. Joshua recognized that breath and knew her nervous system was ready as he leaned in very close to Gweneth and spoke softly.

"I want you to clear your mind of all sensual and sexual thoughts and find a peaceful place where you feel the most content. My voice will move around the room as we begin this meditation. Keep your breathing effortless and focus on my voice." Joshua stood up and quietly moved across the room.
"I want you to imagine that you're sitting in a room, on a white chair with white walls and a single door in front of you. You are safe and you are alone." Joshua paused for several seconds.

"This is your base consciousness. Your safe room." Joshua moved a few more feet to the opposite side of the bed.
"Now, expand the room slowly and manipulate or change it to fit your needs, but don't move from your chair. This is where you live and rest, and the only way into this room is by invitation from you."

Joshua paused and changed position. He lit two candles and retrieved a package of incense from his bag, along with two more candles which he lit and placed strategically around the room.

"Do not share any details about your room with me or anyone else." Joshua continued. "You are the only one who knows what this room looks like, feels like, and it is to be your most closely guarded secret."

Gweneth had not moved and her breathing was remarkably consistent.

After several minutes, Joshua started playing background sounds of a rainforest, with a distant waterfall and different species of creatures communicating in harmony.
"Gweneth, I want you to slowly sit up on the bed and cross your legs." Joshua instructed softly. "Focus on your room, and change the white chair into a cushion or seat you're more comfortable in."

Gweneth sat up and crossed her legs in what seemed to be one choreographed motion. She then stretched her spine and back into a perfect Sukhasana pose, her hands falling to her knees, palms open and up. Joshua lit the incense he pulled from his bag and joined Gweneth on the bed in the same position.

"You are going to change your breathing." Joshua said. "Hold your next breath in and when I tell you to release it, exhale quickly and fully empty your lungs. Keep your eyes closed as I'm going to remove the blindfold." Gweneth held her next breath as Joshua slowly removed the blindfold to reveal two softly closed eyelids, with moderate eye movement underneath. This was an important sign that her conscious mind was present and most likely looking around the room she had created for herself.

"Release your breath fully, then bring life in through your mouth and let that energy flow down between your legs. Visualize that energy leaving your body and flowing up your back, along the outside of your spine. Inhale through your nose, pulling the energy over the top of your head, and back into your body."

Gweneth made several repetitions, visualizing the energy she was breathing in and out, traveling through and all around her.
"I'm going to rest my elbows on your knees and cup my hands together." Joshua said, forming a triangle with his upper body and another by touching his middle and index fingertips as well as the tips of his thumbs. "I want you to rest your forehead in the space between my hands by lowering your head and shifting your weight forward."

Gweneth moved as instructed and the center of her forehead, her third eye and sixth chakra, was positioned within the triangle Joshua was making with his hands.

"Keep breathing in the same pattern and be present in your room." Joshua instructed, as Gweneth followed.

•　•　•　•

Gweneth imagined an orderly room with open space in the middle and a double sided, glass fireplace. She added a very comfortable sofa in the shape of a crescent moon which created an altar-like position for the fireplace.
The lighting was whatever she wanted it to be at any given moment, the colors on the walls matched her mood and were currently shading to reds and greens, reminding her that Christmas wasn't far away.
She did not have a strong visualization of herself in the room, but could see the space she had created through her own eyes.

She could hear Joshua, and knew her physical body was safe and present, but this conscious attempt to see through a different lens was indescribable in her own mind. Gweneth sat on the white suede sofa that was warmed by the heat from the fire and continued breathing.

● ● ● ●

Joshua stayed in the same position with Gweneth for over ten minutes, breathing together and measuring the energy of all of Gweneth's chakras as well as her fertility level. Gweneth's third eye or sixth and seventh chakras were still mostly dormant, however they responded to the energy Gweneth was propelling through and around her body.

"You may sit up Gweneth." Joshua said as he too sat up with very good posture, moving himself closer to Gweneth.
"Open your eyes, and look only into mine." Joshua said.

Gweneth opened her eyes slowly and made direct contact with Joshua's.

"Continue to breathe and try to maintain focus in both my eyes and your room at the same time."
The connection between Joshua and Gweneth was unbreakable. Without the conscious decision to do so, both Gweneth and Joshua came together, forehead to forehead. Their lips, barely touching, formed a bridge for energy to flow from body to body.
Gweneth wrapped her legs around Joshua, sitting between his thighs. His arms were wrapped around Gweneth, his left hand at the top of her back and his right hand on her lower back, cocooning her in divine masculine energy, while she cocooned herself in the pure feminine. Their robe's had opened causing Gweneth's breasts and nipples to caress Joshua's chest as they exchanged breath, eye's still locked.

Joshua's blood was pumping fast through his body and his member was awake, but not fully erect. This journey was for Gweneth to explore a conscious side to her unconscious sexual self. Even though Joshua had completed this same ritual in the past he had never come across personal energy that was as compatible or as strong as Gweneth's.

With little warning, Gweneth took a deeper breath, out of rhythm, and broke eye contact with Joshua. Her eyes rolled back in her head, and her body followed, falling into the sheets and pillow behind her. She arched her back slightly and then quivered as her orgasm echoed through her body. She did not cum and was not physically induced to climax. Gweneth opened up her consciousness to sexual and spiritual energies for the first time and her innocence was disappearing quickly, as her divine feminine was now awake.

Joshua moved to Gweneth's side and spoke slowly, masculine and loving.
"Focus on your breath." Joshua paused and took several personal breaths himself before continuing.
"Let the pleasure you are feeling radiate throughout your body. Feel it at the top of your head and all the way down to the tips of your toes. Lay flat on your back and focus the physical pleasure into your room. Let it shape, design, and mold what you have already created."

Gweneth stretched out her limbs and laid flat on her back. Her eyes had returned to their normal position and her breathing was focused and consistent.
"Oh my God." Gweneth said, searching for more words to describe her experience, however she was at a loss for vocabulary.

"I want you to focus your consciousness and try to stay present in your room." Joshua explained. "That was the first of three releases you must attain. The second and third I will assist with and require delicate body work."

Gweneth closed her eyes and very quickly she found herself back in her room, however the room had changed. The fire was glowing yellow and the heat it radiated was amazing, but not by temperature.

The ceiling was a euphoric shade of blue and blended into the tops of the walls, which were now decorated with sensual and erotic art. On the wall behind the sofa was a mural of a woman's body painted turquoise, and shaded by a large martini glass. The woman's breasts were proudly exposed, however the transparent glass in the shape of a woman's womb distorted everything below and left what was behind the glass to the imagination.

There was a soothing waterfall on her right as she entered. The water was clear but the reflection of blue towards the top, close to the ceiling, changed to an orange pulse of energy as it reached the basin, also in the shape of the female pelvis as a V. Every change about the room Gweneth loved as it felt like a true representation of herself.

Gweneth thought of sitting on the crescent shaped sofa and enjoying the warmth of the fire. Within a blink of an eye she was there. She didn't have to walk across the room or wasn't distracted along the way.

She sat on the sofa and focused on breathing while the passage of time slowed and Gweneth lost herself in the dancing flames of the fireplace.

● ● ● ●

Seconds after Gweneth closed her eyes Joshua began a similar massage as earlier in the morning, however he didn't use oil and his touch was light, engaging Gweneth's nerve endings but not the muscles.

Joshua was moving energy all over Gweneth's body using her first orgasm to perpetuate the opening of her chakras. He changed his motion and held his cupped hands together, hovering over her pelvis, letting her energy build in her lower core.

Slowly, Joshua moved his hands up Gweneth's torso, floating invisible but dense and pure sexual energy up into her stomach, heart and neck. He repeated the motion and included the third eye and top of Gweneth's head as she continued to breathe. She turned slightly to her right, then quivered back to her left and suddenly her knees were bent. Gweneth took another deep breath out of rhythm and let out a very sensual and cleansing sigh.

Her right hand moved from her side to inbetween her legs which spread open like a flower blooming, her feet together, toe to toe and heal to heal.

Gweneth resumed navigating her sexual consciousness on the river of sensual energy, using every area of her vulva and clit to advance closer to her next release.

• • • •

Gweneth didn't feel like she was sitting on the sofa in her room, but rather floating just above the surface. The room had so much more life and ambiance than it did before. She looked around and felt the room was empty, even though vibrant and colorful.

Gweneth sat back on the sofa and stared at the fire, letting it warm her eyes and mind. She inhaled, as if taking a breath, but took in the fire instead. It didn't burn her throat or lungs, however it did give her consciousness a surge of power that radiated through every nerve in her body.

Gweneth felt every energy center ignite starting at the base of her spine, then moving through her womb, charging her genitals and flowing up to her stomach and into her heart. It slowly crawled up the inside of her neck and then above her nose.

The energy moved to the top of her head making her scalp and hair follicles feel tingly and numb. Gweneth felt the top of her head open and the energy left her body flowing up and over her, surrounding her in a sauna of sexual security.

• • • •

Joshua noticed Gweneth's eyes moving quickly under her eyelids. He stopped his motions and watched as Gweneth perpetuated her own journey of sexual discovery. He could feel the energy around her, but it was hers and hers alone.

• • • •

Gweneth didn't close her eyes, but saw only light, like a transition some have described after technically experiencing death. She was physically engaging herself in ways she could have never imagined, but in her mind, Gweneth was in a completely different space.
Light. Just light. Beautiful, endless light.

The brightness subsided and Gweneth recognized the basement of her childhood home. She was eight years old and playing hide and go seek with her older brother Sean, who was twelve. Gweneth hid in a fort made out of four large cushions from a sectional sofa as well as pillows and countless blankets. She was experiencing a memory and could not change her behavior, actions or thoughts. Her consciousness was present in that moment which she could only watch.
Sean jumped from behind the couch, scaring Gweneth. She screamed, he laughed. She began to cry and Sean stopped laughing and sat down to comfort his little sister. After a sincere apology and a prolonged hug, Gweneth felt better, however she also felt something else. She inquired about what was poking her and her brother, embarrassingly told her it was nothing. Gweneth reached at the source of her discomfort and over the next hour she became a victim. He did not penetrate her or physically harm her, as he loved her, but he knew better as he instructed her to keep their playtime a secret and tell no one.
The same type of incident occurred again two months later, and again a month after that. During the final betrayal Sean and Gweneth's father found them, amongst blankets and pillows, discovering what no parent would ever want to see.

From the end of her memory with Sean, Gweneth remembered the

death of her father. He was unable to speak, unable to breathe, and grabbing at his chest, mouth and eyes wide open.
Sean had just turned thirteen and Gweneth was a month away from being nine. Neither Sean nor Gweneth said anything about what had actually caused their father's heart attack, just that he was upset at them for making a mess.
He was pronounced dead when the paramedic's arrived as the EMT that night was also a practicing medical examiner.

Gweneth and Sean did not spend any more time together and hardly spoke after their fathers death. Their mother was inconsolable for weeks and paid little attention to Sean or Gweneth, spending most of her time with the youngest child, four year old Marie.

A year later, Gweneth's mother was getting ready for her first date with a man since becoming a widow when a brutal argument erupted between her mother and now fourteen year old Sean, which had become a more common occurrence.Sean had rage that was uncommon and scary for a boy his age. Sean stormed out of the house and rode off on his bike, leaving his mother on the front porch, asking him not to leave. She canceled her date and waited for Sean to return home.
Sadly, the next time the front door opened it was not Sean, but two police officers with terrible and tragic news.
Gweneth's memory skipped forward to Sean's funeral. It felt like they had buried her father weeks before even though it had been over a year. Gweneth wore the same back dress and sat with her mother who wore a pale, emotionless expression with stone cold eyes and a white complexion, layered with exhaustion.
This poor woman had lost her husband and first born to terrible tragedies that all started when Gweneth's father discovered her doing something physical and inappropriate with her brother.

Shortly after Sean's suicide Gwenth's mother moved them to south Florida to start a new life. Gweneth had suppressed almost all of her memories of her brother and father. This was the largest block Gweneth had to confront from her past. Her consciousness wept for the duration of the recall. Not because of the trauma her brother inflicted on her, but because of the memories she lost that were pure and joyful.

Gweneth now could remember all of what she had lost, or forgotten. Christmas morning when she was six, Sean and her dad teaching her how to ride a bike the following spring. Her parents, together, happy and glowing when they brought her little sister Marie home from the hospital. So many good memories lost and buried with her father and brother.

Gweneth had no conscious recollection of her brother's affections until this point. Now older and with the context of her memories, Gweneth forgave Sean, in her mind and in her soul. She felt he didn't fully understand what he was doing and what he asked her to do. Gweneth did not punish herself as she was eight at the time, and the loss of her father affected her much more significantly.

Gweneth's mind jumped ahead to her sixteenth birthday party. She was wearing a summer dress, which covered a two piece bikini underneath, playing volleyball with her friends on the beach.
A few college students asked if they could join the game. Quickly alliances were formed and the games became quite competitive. One of the college guys flirted with Gweneth and she flirted back, smitten with youthful raging hormones.

After the final game, invitations were extended to Gweneth and her friends to join the collegiate group for dinner at their house just a few hundred yards down the beach. It was an all american menu featuring hotdogs, hamburgers, and beer.
This was the first time Gweneth had been drunk and it was the night she lost her virginity to the college boy she had been flirting with.

He didn't call her the next day and she wasn't expecting him to. For Gweneth, the memory of her first time was perfect. She didn't subscribe to falling in love and losing her virginity in some magical, emotional way. Gweneth thought if she had low or no expectations, and just let it happen, she'd be better off than risk getting her heart broken.

Her first time was next to a small fire on the beach. She was too drunk to drive, but not too drunk to walk, or to give consent in her mind.
The guy was very buff and athletic, but humble and had no trace of ego.
The experience was romantic and sensual. She did not tell him it was her first time as well as not disclosing her real age. All of her friends, including Gweneth, told the older group they were all eighteen and no questions were asked after.

●　●　●　●

Gweneth then found herself in a hot and steamy shower. This setting was not a memory she could recall. She could see her current body, just as if she was fully conscious. Her skin felt soft as if it had been recently washed and the scent of lavender penetrated the billowing steam as Gweneth turned off the water.
She pulled the curtain back and saw a black bath towel hanging on the wall next to the shower. She took the towel from the hook which felt warm and as soft as her skin. Gweneth buried her face in the towel and knew exactly where the lavender was permeating from.

She dried her hair as best she could, wrapped herself in the towel and stepped out into a small bathroom. The dense steam made it difficult to see much detail however she noticed a vanity and a massive mirror above it. There was no toilet and no door. Gweneth did not panic and she knew her body was safe as she was still in her own mind.
The mirror was fogged over as steam kept rising, floating around the small space, however there was no source or cause for the steam.

Gweneth stood at the vanity and noticed her own comb and toothbrush, as well as her favorite body lotion. With her right hand she wiped away the condensation on the mirror and gasped when no reflection was present. This startled her for a few seconds as she considered the possibility she was actually dead.

Gweneth moved her head and body, looking in the mirror for some clue as to where she was. She noticed the shower curtain in the mirror was still closed. She looked to make sure the shower curtain next to her was open. It was. Gweneth looked back in the mirror at the exact moment the shower curtain was slowly pulled open, revealing a familiar body and face.

Gweneth realized she was looking at a version or projection of herself. Her counterpart was glowing beautiful, with intoxicating eyes and an aura around her that was moving, but visually transparent. It was as if the mirror was a lens that let you see the best version of yourself.

Gweneth found her own consciousness feeling self-conscious and secured her towel. Her counterpart noticed Gweneth and smiled. She stepped out of the shower and walked to the mirror, maintaining unshifting eye contact. She spoke first.

"Why are you so shy? She said, smiling and removing the towel that was wrapped around her body, dropping it on the floor. "Be free. Be naked. It's how you came into the world."

"Are you my inner Goddess?" Gweneth asked.

"If you've forgotten, you call me Ashely. Are you going to stand there with a towel on? You know that's going to make this conversation awkward." The young woman in the mirror responded.

Gweneth laughed as she recognized her own brand of humor and she suddenly had a connection to this other part of herself. Gweneth removed her towel, exposing her own body to Ashely.

"See. Don't you feel better?"

"I don't know if I'll remember any of this when I wake up, but this is the weirdest thing I have never thought of. Ashley?"

"We've met once before, very briefly. You liked the idea of using your middle name."

"I'm really confused. What are you supposed to tell me that I don't already know?" Gweneth asked.

"I'm not here to tell you anything except, you should be naked more often." Ashely had a small smile growing from the side of her mouth.

"That's it?" Gweneth repeated. "Then what was all this for? I thought you were supposed to give me some sexual wisdom or insight that would change my life."

"If you remember this conversation when you awake in your conscious body, would you say this experience has changed your life?" She asked.

"Of course." Gweneth started laughing at what she had just said. Her reflection laughed as well.

"Ok. You, we, us - we're one now. You can be me, or this version of yourself, almost anytime you want."

"Almost anytime?" Gweneth asked.

"You have to *want* to release and share your sexual energy, which is the purest form of yourself. If you aren't in the mood or are in a stressful situation, I will be more difficult to summon." Her reflection made reference to the perpetual steam.

"Adrenaline will completely shut down access to this part of yourself in the short term. It acts more like a catalyst in the long term."
She paused and looked at Gweneth who was listening and

studying her own body.

"What's my advantage when I access or use this part of myself?" Gweneth asked, comparing herself to her reflection.

"Influence." Ashley responded. "You will become tired if used a lot in a short amount of time. Just remember to breathe."

"So how do I bring this," Gweneth asked, indicating the steam, "or you into my conscious mind?"

"Just like you did now. Breathing, focus, and finding your way, which will be easier the more you do it."
Ashley licked the tip of her finger and started gently touching her clit. "Arousal is the quickest path, however deep focused meditation works as well."

Gweneth grabbed the edge of the sink as she felt a rush of pleasure between her legs. She looked in the mirror and realized she was feeling what her reflection was inducing.
"This is fucking crazy." Gweneth said.

"Not really. Again, we are one in the same. Imagine, this side of you isn't afraid of anything. Fear locks so many things away. Don't be afraid of being all versions of yourself." Ashley stopped, noticing the steam dissipating.

"Notice how there's less steam." She indicated to Gweneth who looked around and could tell there was noticeably less.
"That's a sign that you're running low on energy. We'll talk again soon. Time to wake up." Ashley took a few steps back.

"Wait!" Gweneth said, trying to think of one more question, to try and get one more answer.

"It's ok. We'll play more later. Just breathe and *wake up!*" Ashley said, reaching out and pointing at Gweneth who immediately woke and found herself on the bed in the hotel room with Joshua, remembering everything for the second time.

CHAPTER 4

Tuesday, 10:26pm

Gweneth laid on the bed, exhausted, staring up at the ceiling. Joshua sat across the room, watching Gweneth process everything she had experienced over the last twenty hours.

Gweneth projected her voice in the same direction she was staring.

"I still don't quite understand what this energy or power that I have is? How do I use it?"

Joshua responded, somber and also exhausted.

"Think about Cleopatra. She had incredible influence, was mysteriously exotic and quite public in her seduction and control of men. In addition to seducing Julius Caesar and Mark Antony, she controlled her father, two brothers and eventually her son. She ruled ancient Egypt for over thirty years." Joshua paused.
"You can persuade just about anybody to do just about anything, and with less energy than most with the same skill set. I also believe that you are a much better person than Cleopatra."

"If I want to use this ability, I have to meditate and become aroused?" Gweneth asked.

"Initially, yes." Joshua sat up in his chair. "It all starts with breathing and it does become easier each time. Just like learning how to develop any new muscle memory." Joshua looked down at the floor and then back to Gweneth, although her visual focus was still on the ceiling.

"If you use that side of yourself a lot, eventually, the two sides will merge and truly become one consciousness. It does take more physical energy from your body to sustain a high level of neuroelectric conversion, so if your body is tired it will become difficult to focus."

"That's why I woke up." Gweneth responded, still staring at the ceiling. "I really don't know what to think of all this. On one hand, it's really fucking cool, but on the other hand, I'm not sure about what I'm supposed to do with it. I'd rather focus on enjoying and expanding my knowledge of this new sexual world."

Joshua stood up and went directly into the bathroom. He closed the door and turned on the faucet, splashing cold water on his face. He looked at himself in the mirror and took two deep intensional breaths.

He looked tired and worried. There was only one more phase to complete Gweneth's initial programming. Joshua was reluctant in how he was told to proceed. He knew the final step would ensure that Gweneth's sexual consciousness would become the more dominant voice in her head and, as a result, her own life would certainly end far sooner.

Joshua came out of the bathroom and drew Gweneth's attention as he opened the curtains and walked out on the patio once more. He didn't look at her or signal her to follow him, but quickly moved as far away from the room as possible.

Gweneth followed and walked up behind Joshua, wrapping her arms around his waist, his attention focused out towards the Atlantic Ocean.

"Something's wrong." Gweneth whispered. "I can sense fear and your struggle with something. What is it?"

Joshua turned his head and looked at Gweneth's beautiful face and warm eyes. "Everything is fine." Joshua said. "I'm just tired." Joshua knew the room was being monitored with video and audio surveillance. He didn't know who was watching, and if they knew how valuable Gweneth was.

Joshua turned his body and returned the embrace, kissing Gweneth's forehead then whispered in her ear.

"You're right, but we can't talk here." Joshua paused and looked Gweneth in the eyes. She could tell right away he was worried and telling the truth.

He kissed her deeply then returned to the embrace and whispered in her ear again, kissing her neck every few words. "I know you trust me."

Kiss. "I need to do something a little unorthodox and it might," *kiss*, " put you in a bit of danger, but you'll be in far greater danger," *kiss*, " if I don't."

Joshua pulled back and looked back into Gweneth's eyes, to make sure it didn't appear as if he was whispering, not knowing who could be watching. She understood and didn't give any visual sign indicating she heard what he said, but he saw Gweneth's answer in her eyes.

Joshua kissed her deeply again and then asked, "Are you ready for the last phase?"

"I am." Gweneth said. "This phase doesn't, by chance, involve sleeping?"

"No, the opposite in fact." Joshua responded with a shy grin. He walked back into the suite, this time with Gweneth behind him, hand in hand.

Gweneth excused herself to the bathroom and Joshua opened a bottle of water from the refrigerator in the satellite kitchen. He then retrieved the small envelope from his robe pocket and tapped out two small pills onto the counter top.

Each tablet was about the size of a baby aspirin with no stamp or label. One was white, the other pink, and could easily be swallowed or crushed and dissolved in someone's drink. Joshua had no such plans. Gweneth came out from the bathroom and stood at the counter top, noticing the water and two small pills.

"What are those?"

"It's a combination of different compounds." Joshua explained. "Typically, for this final phase, I would dissolve this one in orange juice or tea without showing you first." Joshua paused and looked at a spot on the ceiling. Gweneth followed his gaze and noticed a very small camera, well concealed within the ceiling.

"Since you have progressed so quickly and seem to be a natural, I'm taking a big risk showing you these and asking that you take them willingly."

"What do they do?" Gweneth asked.

"This one is a mild psychotropic combined with scopolamine, which makes you susceptible to direct influence."

Joshua pointed to the pink pill. "This one helps relax the body, and speed up the mind. There's not a name for it yet and it's proprietary to Redhawk. It helps solidify the progress we've made over the last twenty hours."

"Making certain experiences more permanent?" Gweneth asked.

"Yes, that's the result in most cases." Joshua walked over to the nightstand next to the bed and retrieved the piece of paper he had folded and set aside earlier. It was the three most important things in Gweneth's life when she first arrived in Joshua's hotel room. "Remember writing these?"

"Yes." Gweneth said. "Although it seems like it's been a lot longer than early this morning."

Joshua unfolded the stationary and read the listed items then handed the paper to Gweneth. "Are these still the three most important things in your life?" Joshua asked.

Gweneth refolded it without reading it, remembering what she had written down. "Yes they are."

"Then you should take these." Joshua said, staring into Gweneth's eyes, again, non-verbally asking for trust.
"Take this one now." He said, indicating the white pill, "And then in a few hours you'll take the other."

Gweneth picked up the small white pill with her thumb and index finger and looked back into Joshua's eyes which were reassuring. She put the pill in the middle of her tongue and took a big sip of water. Gweneth swallowed, took a breath, and finished the water with another long gulp.

"Now what?" Gweneth asked, looking a little nervous.

"Remember the massage I gave you early this morning?" Joshua insinuated she might be getting the same treatment again.

"Of course." Gweneth said with a smile, eyebrows raised in anticipation.

"Now it's your turn to give the massage." Joshua replied, forming a shy smile with the corner of his mouth.

Gweneth, not disappointed but unfamiliar with actual massage techniques, lowered one of her eyebrows enough to ask the question in her mind, 'Do I know how to give a sensual massage?'

"I'll do my best." She said with a smile.
"The key for beginning this exercise is to control your breathing with each massage stroke. Once you feel grounded, try to access your room while continuing to breathe and let the energy in your body guide your hands. Don't think about the massage. React to what my energy is guiding you to do." Joshua explained. "Once you find your room, the rest will take care of itself."

He walked over to the balcony door and closed the curtains then proceeded to relight the candles in the room, helping set the mood.

Joshua took off his robe exposing his masculine body. His penis wasn't hard, but was not limp or retracted. Gweneth walked over to him and put her hands on his chest.

"How soon will I start to feel the effects of what I just took?" She asked.

"If you find your room quick enough, you won't feel any effects. However, you'll be able to maintain a connection, and be present with your Goddess longer."

Gweneth pushed her body up, pressing against Joshua's. She stood on the balls of her feet and kissed him sensually. She lowered herself, kissing the base of his neck, his chest, and around his nipples. She untied her robe and let the front fall open, exposing her stomach and more of her breasts. Gweneth put her head against his heart and consciously started breathing. His skin was warm and she could feel his chest moving in and out in the same rhythm as her own.

Joshua laid face down on the bed as Gweneth slowly ran the tips of her fingers across his shoulders and down his back, legs, and ankles. She added massage oil to his lower body and tightened her grip on Joshua's legs, one in each hand, moving blood through the muscles, up into Joshua's core. She engaged the nerves in Joshua's lower back with moderate pressure and then worked the blood and subsequent energy from his arms and shoulders, directing it towards his first and second chakras. Gweneth took conscious breaths with each intentional movement and started to feel herself relax.

She thought about her experience receiving all of this information and sensory input over the past day. She recalled her dream of soaring over the earth, viewing everything from far above, at a distance where you can't help but see a different perspective.

Gweneth closed her eyes and continued breathing. The last time she found her room more sexually embellished and she wondered if the decor and artwork would remain the same. Being that it was her room, it would have whatever decor and ambiance she desired, or so she tried to make herself believe.

Her thoughts of dancing through clouds and riding thermals over mountain tops was where her mind took her. With her eyes closed, she felt weightless in her mind. She stopped thinking about the massage and about Joshua. She was flying!

Gweneth could not tell if she was a bird, or if she was in her own body, gracefully penetrating the atmosphere. Her journey of flight led her high above the trees, clouds, and pollution of the populus. Once above the noise, Gweneth heard true silence for the first time.

As she descended, she felt a tear fall away from her eye as she wept at the beauty of the Earth. Gweneth descended quickly through the clouds and found herself circling a small island.

She glided over the sea and approached a beautiful and vacant beach just a few hundred feet below. Passing over the white sand and crystal blue water, a coastal thermal carried Gweneth over a bank of dense trees and into a valley, lush with vegetation. Less than a hundred feet above the surface Gweneth spotted a narrow stream flowing opposite her direction.

Her angle of attack dropped her just above the water's surface. Moving quickly, she came upon the bottom of a tall waterfall flowing from two hundred feet above. Her momentum didn't change and she moved through the falling curtain of water, not feeling one drop on her body. There was a cave behind the waterfall which became increasingly smaller, the deeper she traveled.

The cave soon became a narrow tunnel and Gweneth seemed to be walking, instead of floating, however she could not see her feet or legs. The tunnel narrowed until it was only wide enough for a single person to get through. Gweneth found herself at the top of a red winding staircase, curling down almost thirty feet, ending at a stone wall with a single door.

The door was illuminated with a single sconce with amber light flowing upwards. The door had three letters carved in it, evenly spaced across the width of the door. G.A.C.

Gweneth, recognizing her own initials, reached for the handle and immediately passed through the door into her space, which was just the way she remembered it. The glowing water fountain, the mural of the turquoise breasted woman, and the extravagant fireplace. That's when Gweneth noticed the fire. It wasn't nearly as intense or penetrating as before.

Gweneth didn't understand why the fire wasn't as hot, or why this experience was different than her first journey to this conscious sexual security blanket.

She found herself on the couch in front of the fireplace, breathing and focusing on the flames as she had done before. After what felt like an hour, there was still no change in the strength or girth of the fire, as Gweneth's focus was wavering. She gazed around the room and noticed a mirror and vanity tucked away behind her, perpendicular to the fireplace. This time she didn't move by thought. Instead, she stood up and moved through the room normally, recognizing the vanity as she got closer.

It was the same space she had encountered her inner goddess. Gweneth looked in the mirror and saw her own reflection, however, the room was not reflected behind her. Gweneth looked to her left and saw the shower she had been in before, but something was missing.

'The steam,' Gweneth thought.

The fire and steam were both sources of heat and power, which Gweneth seemed to be lacking.

'What is different?' She thought. She considered the pill she had taken, physical exhaustion, and the last time she was physically navigating her own body, as now she was navigating Joshua's.

Gweneth looked in the shower but could not find anything that would turn the water on. She focused back on her reflection in the mirror and continued to breathe. Gweneth closed her eyes, choosing to breathe in darkness.

This time she did not count the minutes, or hours, or any passage of time. She only existed, breath by breath.

Gweneth imagined taking a hot, relaxing shower. She could feel the water hitting her neck, warming her spine, and trickling down the small of her back. She felt the kiss of steam on her face and in her nose. She felt heat rising up from beneath her like it had before.

Gweneth opened her eyes and found herself in the exact position she had imagined. She was standing in the shower with steam starting to fill the room.

With her eyes open, she imagined the temperature of the water becoming hotter, almost to the point of burning.

After a few breaths the water got much hotter, startling Gweneth and giving her the slightest perception of pain. This trigger ignited her just like after the first ritual Joshua performed. Gweneth's primal urge to mate was strong and the steam continued building until there was no longer water, just steam.

Gweneth couldn't help but touch herself. Just as she had experienced in her physical body, her Goddess was calling her. The idea of resisting never crossed Gweneth's mind.

Floating in a cloud of warmth, the shower and vanity had disappeared, and only the mirror remained. Gweneth had one hand sensually working her clit and circling lower, probing with the tips of her fingers. It wasn't teasing, but channeling energy exactly where she wanted it.

Her other hand was caressing her breasts and stomach. The mirror cleared enough for Gweneth's reflection to change positions and ask one question.

"Looks like fun. Can I come play?"

Gweneth didn't answer. She looked in Ashley's eyes and imagined her crawling through the mirror, but the transition wasn't quite as dramatic. Ashley smiled and the reflection went back to Gweneth's perception of herself. After two quick blinks, Gweneth took a deep breath in and her eyes closed. She felt a change in her physiology and quickly all her inhibitions, insecurities, and reservations vanished. Her posture straightened and her pulse quickened. It was like being drunk, but not intoxicated or foolish. Gweneth opened her eyes however the reflection, both physically and emotionally was Ashley. The mirror was now a portal to her physical body. A smile emerged from Ashley's lips that would give even the most committed man a moment of pause. Ashley slowly closed her eyes and thought of Joshua. She took one deep, focused breath, opened her eyes, and found her body pressed against his.

●　　●　　●　　●

Joshua was still laying on his stomach, his arms spread out to his sides, almost stretching the width of the bed. Ashley continued the massage where Gweneth left off. The robe Gweneth was wearing was now tossed aside as she was using her whole body to stimulate Joshua's.

Ashley whispered in Joshua's ear. "Are you ready for me?"

Joshua's eyes opened and he knew what was about to happen, or at least he thought he did. The voice that came out of Ashley was distinguishable from Gweneth in depth, tone, and confidence.

When Gweneth had met Joshua in his hotel room, she had been under an induced hypnosis to bring her Goddess out, although for a very short time. By Gweneth inviting her own Goddess into her conscious mind, the transformation is stronger and cannot be broken by a code word, or normal hypnosis technique. Joshua's concern was once the second drug was in her system, Ashley would become the primary personality and Gweneth would be locked away, eventually becoming unrecoverable.

Joshua rolled over as Ashley rocked back, sitting with her legs together and knees bent. As Joshua straightened himself out, Ashley rocked forward with her hands on the bed, moving like a cat getting ready to pounce. Joshua's member was hard and grew harder as Ashely approached it.

He was expecting her to take him in her mouth like Gweneth did earlier, however her gaze was locked on Joshua's eyes rather than his penis. She prowled right over his throbbing member. It grazed her breast and nipple then tickled her ribs and stomach as she mounted him. She straddled his ribcage, dripping wetness onto his chest. Ashley looked deep into Joshua's eyes. Her right hand was palm down, covering Joshua's heart, and her voice was like music, soft, passionate, yet strong and feminine at the same time.

Joshua said nothing. He was mesmerized by Ashley and in shock she manifested herself so quickly. By his estimate, Gweneth had started the massage thirty minutes prior to Ashley greeting him. Joshua focused on his own breathing inhaling deeply through his nose. Her scent, dripping on his chest, filled his nostrils, penetrating his body. It was potent and pleasant, his mind racing to define it. It had a lure of sweetness, just like her voice, which made you want to inhale more. Once deep inside his body it felt warm like red wine, and with several breaths, one would quickly give into complete inebriation.

At that point, Joshua thought about the second pill provided by the company. He never planned on Gweneth taking it and ending up like the other young women who worked for Redhawk Marketing. He now had a plan of his own and hoped like hell he was right. Joshua had never met anyone whose influence was as potent or accessible as Gweneth's. He knew, from this point forward, he was in over his head.

● ● ● ●

Joshua and Ashley fucked for over two hours. Their bond was not romantic or sensual this time. It was rough and animalistic, both of them taking turns dominating the other. The kisses that opened the gates to this sexual energy were now bites and slobber, sweat and aggression. There weren't any permanent marks left on their bodies, however Ashley left proof that she won the battle as Joshua could feel a few bite marks still throbbing on different areas of his body.

Ashley consumed every last drop Joshua had and laid her head on his chest. She listened to his beating heart, which sounded strong. Ashley looked at Joshua and smiled, speaking for the first time in three hours.

"I'm going to go take a shower, alone this time." Ashley stood up, leaving Joshua exposed and limp. His breathing was more like panting, begging for energy while Ashley stood before him, equally exposed and effortlessly breathing in perfect rhythm.

"What time is it?" Joshua asked.

"Four a.m." Ashley replied, walking into the bathroom and starting the water. "Can you call the front desk and have them bring a few more dry towels?" Even though Ashley asked Joshua, her tone suggested it wasn't a question.

Joshua sat up on the side of the bed and reached for the phone to call the front desk and was startled when it immediately rang. Joshua took a deep conscious breath and answered the phone. "Hello."

He recognized the voice on the other end immediately. It was Trish Blackman.

"Susan would like to see you and Ashley in her office in thirty minutes. Room 6015." Joshua looked up at the ceiling, knowing Susan's office was directly above them.

Trish continued. "Have Ashley come up first, then you, ten minutes later."

"Understood." Joshua responded, followed by a click from the other end.

Joshua took another deep breath and called the front desk. He asked for two towels and three packets of aspirin sold in the hotel guest pantry. He bribed the front desk attendant with a twenty dollar tip if he could get it to the room in less than five minutes.

Joshua had not given Gweneth the drug that would make Ashley the more dominant personality, however he was positive Susan would test her blood guaranteeing her investment was now insured.
If the drug was not in her system, Gweneth would either be dismissed from the program, or they would try again with a different programmer and most likely succeed. In either scenario, Joshua knew this would be his last test, which meant a strong chance he could be dead within a few days. This meant there was a very slim chance he could save his daughter and disappear before the company could find them.

Joshua stood up from the bed and put on a pair of sweatpants from his suitcase and a hoodie from the closet. He washed his face in the kitchen sink and dried it with a dish towel which he tossed on the counter. Joshua took a few deep breaths and tried to calm his mind. He meticulously imagined the course of events over the next few hours and opened his eyes.

He walked to the desk across from the bed and retrieved a $20 bill from his wallet. He took two more deep breaths, walked to the door and opened it with the front desk agent only three steps away, towels and aspirin in hand.

• • • •

Ashley stood in the shower letting the water run from the top of her head down her shoulders and back. She felt her strength weakening and her physical body exhausted. She thought of Joshua's face while she was riding him and how it changed when he was engaging her from behind.

His hand was entangled in her hair holding her head, slightly turned so she could watch him thrust himself deep into her and pull out slowly just to thrust again. Each instance his pulsing head would hit her G-spot like a hammer, then caress it softly before hitting it again.

Ashley smiled at the memory and even felt a slight tingle between her legs which made her smile wider.

Without warning, Ashley let out an uncontrollable yawn, opening her throat and taking in a large amount of air. She closed her eyes as the yawn perpetuated itself and continued for longer than any other yawn she could remember.

She lowered her head and as the yawn subsided, she felt tired and drained. As she opened her eyes her smile returned remembering the last thought going through her mind before the yawn. Then a rush of self doubt, anxiety, and fear. Another deep breath followed, without a yawn.

"Oh my." Gweneth said out loud to herself, now with a better understanding of the purpose of the ritual.

Gweneth finished her shower and was staring into the mirror in the bathroom. There was steam in the air and Gweneth kept looking at her reflection, expecting to see or talk to Ashley, but she only saw her own reflection, imperfections and all.

She remembered everything that happened while Ashley was in control, but she felt a barrier, not allowing her to emotionally connect to what she physically remembered. Gweneth took a deep breath and let out an exhaustive sigh.

A knock at the bathroom door startled her and it started to open.

"Come in." Gweneth responded as Joshua was walking into the bathroom.

He stopped as soon as he saw Gweneth, perfectly nude, looking beautiful and innocent, and obviously not Ashley.

"Gweneth." He said, smiling, handing her a towel. "How do you feel?"

Gweneth blushed, but didn't turn away or look down. She took one step towards Joshua and kissed him with soft lips and deep gratitude.

"I feel ok." She paused. "Good. I feel good, but I'm totally spent." Gweneth smiled and looked relaxed. "Please tell me it's ok to get some sleep."
Joshua looked at Gweneth with awe and hope, knowing this could be the last time he was with the real Gweneth. Joshua wanted to stretch every second out to remember her as this person and goddess before him.

"You're amazing." Joshua said, looking directly into her eyes.

Gweneth tilted her head sideways and the ends of her wet hair followed gravity and fell from her shoulder, dripping a few drops onto the floor before she started wrapping her hair in the towel. This was it. The moment, the scent, the image, the feeling in his stomach and the tiny hairs standing up on the back of his neck. This was the exact moment Joshua fell in love with Gweneth.

CHAPTER 5

Wednesday, 4:08 am

Joshua understood love better than most people. He connected emotions and inner psyche with the conscious mind and physical body. Joshua believed that being with someone physically, emotionally, or spiritually could all be achieved individually, or in different combinations, with different intensities. His research found that couples with consistent intensities in their energy patterns were more stable, and both partners felt secure in their relationship. The same research also showed that couples with higher variations in their energy patterns have less security and trust. Over time these patterns could lead one or both partners to stray outside of the relationship.

Joshua had not dated or pursued any long term romantic interests since the birth of his only daughter. He enjoyed a few casual relationships but had not maintained any sexual encounters outside of the women he helped program for the company, over the last nine months. Gweneth was the seventh candidate he had worked with and she would be the last, by his own decision. Gweneth was the first woman who generated these types of emotions for Joshua since before the birth of his daughter, Erin. Joshua looked at Gweneth and could see her physical exhaustion. Knowing the timing and luck they needed, he kept his spark of emotion to himself.

"You'll be able to sleep soon." Joshua whispered in Gweneth's ear. "But for the next two hours, there are a lot of things that have to go right."

Joshua leaned back and spoke in a more normal volume. "Susan would like to see you in her office in fifteen minutes. I'll be there shortly after."

"Really? Why?" Gweneth asked.

"Our ritual is finished." Joshua explained. "Susan probably wants to have a conversation and see how you're feeling." He gave Gweneth a close hug and whispered in her ear again.
"She wants to talk to Ashley."

Gweneth whispered back into Joshua's ear. "I'm exhausted. I don't know if..."

"I'll help you. Trust me, it will be fine." Joshua interrupted, still whispering. He handed Gweneth four small aspirin.
"Take these, it's just aspirin. It will help. I wish we had more time and more privacy to explain, but the last few hours have gotten away from me." Joshua said, smiling.

Gweneth filled a small glass with water and swallowed the aspirin. "Now what?"

"Get dressed. Breathe and find your room." Joshua handed Gweneth the oil he used during her first massage. "This oil is fused with a very diluted form of LSD. It helps sensitivity and neuro-" Joshua stopped. "Doesn't matter. Use a little bit to help navigate your way back. Oh, you probably shouldn't wear panties."

"Why?" Gweneth asked.

"Ashley wouldn't." Joshua started the water in the shower and undressed. "I'm going to take a quick shower and will be out in a few minutes." Gweneth had the thought of joining him and took that as a sign to excuse herself.

Gweneth towel dried the rest of her body. She brushed her hair while looking at herself in a familiar mirror. The woman she saw before her was not the same woman she saw twenty-six hours earlier. She wasn't looking at Ashley, nor was she looking for her. Gweneth was admiring herself and almost laughed at the notion that she thought she wasn't strong enough to accomplish her dreams. In that moment, she remembered the pain she had been carrying for so long, but was now free from. Free as a bird gliding, watching, and soaring as purpose.

Gweneth put on her dress and gathered the few things she had with her, all of which fit in a small, strapless purse. She heard the water in the shower stop as she sat down in the chair. Gweneth closed her eyes and focused her breath on her lower chakras, trying to restart an exhausted engine.

Suddenly there was a knock at the hotel room door. Gweneth's eyes shot open as she froze for only a moment. Unsure if she should open it she thought to herself, 'What would Ashely do?'

Gweneth opened the door where a shorter and unimpressive man stood in front of her. She recognized him from the NLP conference the previous night. He was wearing a salmon colored polo, tucked into pressed blue jeans. He was not expecting Gweneth to open the door and seemed unsure he had the right room.

"Can I help you?" Gweneth asked, remembering she had met him before.

The man at the door was trying to look around Gweneth, visually searching the room.

"I'm sorry. I might have the wrong room number." He said, seeming embarrassed.
As he turned to walk away Joshua emerged from the bathroom drying his hair and with a towel wrapped around his waist. The man stopped and turned back towards the room. His expression of embarrassment turned to one of shock, then quickly anger and

disappointment.

"Josh." The man said.

Joshua stopped drying his hair and for a brief moment shared the same look of shock as the man at the door.

"Paul." Joshua said, unsure of what to say next.

"I know this isn't a good time." Paul muttered, obviously holding back emotion. He looked at Gweneth and then back at Joshua. "I know you're normally up early." He stopped and was looking towards the floor, avoiding eye contact.
Paul started to walk away and stopped again. He turned half way around and looked back at Joshua.
"I'm going to catch an earlier flight. I'll meet you in Chicago." Paul headed back down the hallway towards the elevators.

Joshua stepped out of the room and took a few strides down the hallway to try to offer Paul some explanation of why a beautiful, half naked coed was in his hotel room at 4:15am. As Joshua passed the room next to his he noticed a short female figure getting off the elevator at the end of the hallway. Paul was halfway between Joshua and the woman who Joshua recognized immediately.

Paul noticed Joshua following and slowed, wanting to have a conversation without Gweneth standing in front of them. Joshua, knowing what was truly at stake, made a decision he never thought he'd have to make.
He stopped, extended his hand towards Paul and half smiled.
"I'll see you in Chicago." Joshua said, then quickly turned and disappeared into his room, Gweneth still standing just inside.
Joshua didn't have time to explain anything to Paul. Joshua looked at Gweneth who was staring back at him, her expression asking for guidance. He took a step toward Gweneth and wrapped his arm around her hip, looking deep into her eyes.

"Ashley." Joshua said, blinking twice. "Ashley, when I come out of the bathroom I need you to grab me and kiss me like she isn't here."

Joshua then turned and was two steps into the bathroom as Trish Blackman stepped into Gweneth's view.

"Good morning." Trish said, announcing herself.

"Good morning." Gweneth tried her best to think and act as her inner Goddess would. She smiled and looked Trish up and down. "I like your outfit."
Gweneth looked into Trisha's eyes and touched the lapel on the suit jacket she was wearing. "You'll let me borrow it sometime?"

Trish was caught off guard enough to slightly blush and take a step back. She extended her right hand to re-introduce herself. "I'm Trish Blackman. You must be Ashley?"

"I've never left this room and yet people have already heard of me. I remember you." Gweneth smiled. "Lobby, elevator, Susan's assistant, and the hotel room before the conference."

"Good memory. Speaking of Susan, she would like to see you upstairs." Trish spoke very professionally, almost robotic in a way. Gweneth then realized that there was a good possibility Trish was also exposed to some form of influence.

She noticed her very subtle breathing pattern and her eye movement didn't seem completely natural. Gweneth decided to push a boundary since Joshua had not yet returned.
She took one step toward Trish and whispered softly in her ear. "We have time, if you want to come in and play. Joshua won't mind. We could surprise him." Gweneth parched her lips and blew a sensual column of air on Trish's neck, below her ear.

Gweneth saw the tiny hairs on the back of Trish's neck rise and a slight quiver shook Trish enough to almost consider the advance. Trish took one more step back, away from Gweneth.

"We actually don't have time." Trish said, blushing more. "Susan is waiting for us and she has travel plans early this morning."

Joshua appeared from the bathroom holding a glass of water, still wrapped in the towel from the waist down. "Good morning." He said, looking directly at Trish.

Gweneth turned and took two steps towards Joshua, wrapping one of her legs around his, her dress rising enough on her thigh to reveal she wasn't wearing panties.
"I invited her in but she said no." Gweneth said, staring into Joshua's eyes. She took a deep breath and then pressed her lips to his.
She felt his tongue squeeze between her lips and she opened her mouth, inviting him in. The kiss was deep and passionate and started to make her wet again. Just before he pulled away Joshua passed Gweneth something from his mouth to hers. It didn't feel like a pill, but a small dry cotton ball. Joshua transferred the small object with enough saliva that Gweneth could swallow it, but turned her head after breaking the kiss, so her swallow wouldn't be obvious.

Joshua tried to distract Trish, who was seemingly unphased by their kiss.
"Are you sure you don't want to come in for a few minutes?" Joshua asked.

Trish, seeming even more confused, appeared to be losing her patients. "Mr. Miller, I need Ms. Ashley upstairs right away." Trish started walking down the hallway. "Ashley, please come with me."
"I'll grab my purse." Gweneth said. She retreated into the room, picked up her purse and headed for the door.

Joshua handed her the glass of water. "Drink."

Gweneth whispered. "What did I swallow?"

"Drink. It's nothing that you'll feel, but it's what Susan will test you for. I crushed a small piece and wrapped it in tissue. It will get into your bloodstream faster. That's why I had you take the aspirin." Gweneth took a large sip of water and handed the glass back to Joshua.

"Try to stall as long as you can. I'll meet you upstairs soon and remember to breathe." Joshua was interrupted by Trish from just outside the door.

"Ms. Ashley, I really do insist we go. Now."

"Coming!" Gweneth said, cheerful and unaffected by Trish's uncompromising attitude. She kissed Joshua's cheek and whispered. "See you soon."

Gweneth walked down the hallway a few steps behind Trish and it was obvious they had moved past pleasantries and social etiquette. Gweneth was getting used to breathing consciously, however breathing consciously and walking at the same time was more challenging. She focused on her posture and with each breath, searched for her room, eyes open, mind adrift.

As the elevator doors closed, so did Gweneth's eyes. Her focus was on her breath and finding what little energy she had left. Trish did not say a word and continued to look straight ahead. There was tension between them, however it didn't seem to bother either Trish or Gweneth. The elevator rose one floor and Gweneth followed Trish from the elevator down the hall. Gweneth felt a spark during her kiss with Joshua and imagined that spark growing hotter with every step.

It seemed like a longer walk down the same hallway for Gweneth. They didn't stop at room 6015, rather continued to room 6017. As Trish approached the door it opened from the inside. Trish walked in with Gweneth now four steps behind, not showing any urgency. As Gweneth entered the room she noticed a nicely dressed man holding the door open and the scent of cherry. The lighting was dim and Susan laid on a king size bed, covering herself with a dark purple silk robe.

"What are you most afraid of?" Susan asked.

Gweneth smiled, recalling her question to Joshua the night before.

"I'm not afraid of anything." Gweneth spoke with as much confidence and swagger as possible, looking Susan directly in the eyes. She smiled and asked Susan the same question.
"What are you most afraid of, Susan?"

Susan nodded slowly, acknowledging Ashely's choice of response with a 'well played' gesture. Her presents didn't seem as commanding or executive as before.

"There's a lot to be afraid of in this world." Susan's tone was strong but quiet. "That's why I'm glad you're working with us." She smiled, patting the side of the bed. "Come sit down and tell me about your evening."

Gweneth almost asked if she could use the bathroom, however, she realized Ashley wasn't the type to ask permission.
"I will elaborate all you like, however, I must use your bathroom. I was rushed up here before I had the opportunity to go." She smiled at Trish who was standing quietly off to the side, next to the unfamiliar man in the dark suit.
Gweneth looked back at Susan as she walked to the bathroom. "Don't worry. I won't be long."

Gweneth was trying to read Susan's body language but everything about her seemed open and unsuspecting. Gweneth closed the door to the bathroom and sat down on the toilet with little urge to pee. She closed her eyes and imagined the river and waterfall concealing the location of her room. She felt a slight stream of urine and started breathing more rhythmically. Her steam intensified and the hairs on her arms and neck stood up. As Gweneth purged what little hydration she had left, the river and waterfall seemed more within reach.

Gweneth stood up, turned on the water and looked in the mirror. She closed her eyes and took two more deep breaths, feeling energy flow up her spine. Upon opening her eyes Gweneth noticed her reflection's eyes were still closed.

Gweneth wasn't in her room, which is the only place she had seen Ashley's reflection. She was positive she was conscious and in her own body. Gweneth peered closer to the mirror, waiting for Ashley to suddenly open her eyes, but she didn't. Ashley's eyes remained closed and her breathing was indicative of sleep.

Gweneth thought to herself, 'Out of everything that has happened to me tonight, this might be the strangest.'
As much as she wanted to study her sleeping reflection, Gweneth knew Susan would become suspicious if she took much longer. She washed her hands and opened the door. A quick glance back at the mirror revealed her true reflection, which made Gweneth smile. Walking back into the suite Gweneth stood tall, walking with confidence, and ready to engage in whatever test Susan had planned.
As Gweneth turned the corner she was surprised to see Susan standing at the foot of the bed, completely dressed with Trish helping her put on a light weight jacket. The door adjoining the office suite with the bedroom was open and the dark suited man was in the office on the phone, speaking a language Gweneth was not familiar with.

"I'm sorry Ashley, we have to cut our meeting short." Susan turned and was handed something by Trish. "I've received some news that requires my immediate attention. May I see your hand?"

Gweneth, unsure if Susan was suspicious of her or Joshua, responded as she felt Ashley would.
"I hope it's not anything too serious." Gweneth extended her right hand.

Susan took Gweneth's hand in hers, feeling the tops of her fingers, then flipping her hand over, looking at her palm. Susan took what looked like a white staple remover and clamped it over Gweneth's index finger. A quick prick of her finger could have startled Gweneth from breaking character, however she was expecting something.

"I could have guessed you were a sadist." Gweneth smiled.

Susan only raised her eyes and showed no emotion. She removed the finger clamp from Gweneth's finger and then pulled a piece of film from the clamp. Susan put the clamp in her pocket and handed the film to Trish who disappeared into the office.

"You'll be surprised at what you learn about yourself over the next few years." Susan said, changing subjects quickly. "The situation is quite serious, hence my early departure. However it's nothing you need to worry about. You've had a very exciting and exhausting two days and I want you to go home, get some rest, and start packing."

"Packing?" Gweneth questioned.

"Our last surprise, for today." Susan stopped and turned, looking at Trish who gave Susan a very slight nod, confirming the company's drug was in Gweneth's system.

"There will be a moving truck outside your apartment Friday morning at 8:00am. Check your email. You will receive instructions for your next training assignment. Friday night, be ready."

Trish returned from the office carrying Gweneth's gym bag with her clothes and personal belongings. She set it on the bed as Susan continued.
"Take a few minutes to change into something less sensual. We don't want to draw unnecessary attention to ourselves." Susan cracked half a smile. "I'm glad you're here. I know you won't disappoint me." She turned and started to exit through the office suite.

"When will I see you again?" Gweneth asked.

"Soon enough." Susan walked out the office suite door into the hallway with the man in the black suit following close behind her.

Suddenly, it was only Gweneth and Trish in the room. Gweneth opened her gym bag and everything was just as she had left it. The pantsuit she arrived in along with a pair of blue jeans and a sweatshirt were neatly folded and her $20,000 check was laying across the top.

Her cell phone, car keys and billfold were in the inside pocket, seemingly undisturbed. Gweneth pulled the blue jeans and sweatshirt from the bag and laid them on the bed.

Trish spoke inquisitively, breaking the tension between them for the first time.
"I want you to know that I'm not your enemy, or your competition." Trish paused and took a step closer towards Gweneth along with a noticeably deeper breath. "I'm curious. What's it like?"

"What's what like?" Gweneth asked.

"Your transformation was easier than most. I have tried several times to connect with my inner Goddess, without success." Trish lowered her head slightly embarrassed. "Your connection took minutes in comparison, and the difference is quite obvious."

Gweneth felt herself start to blush at what seemed like a compliment. She took a deep breath and looked at Trish without responding. Gweneth subdued her breathing and took two steps toward Trish, this time she did not retreat. Gweneth reached at the sides of her dress and pulled it over her head, exposing her confident and beautiful naked body.

Trish blushed and looked down, silent and nervous. Gweneth noticed how Trish was breathing. It wasn't smooth or rhythmic as it had been, and Gweneth could now feel what Joshua had been talking about. Her energy was stronger than Trish's energy at this moment. Gweneth could feel Trish's energy submit to hers. Physically, Trish was submitting through her body language and tone.

With her index and middle fingers, Gweneth lifted Trish's head by her chin, regained eye contact, and slowly pressed her lips to Trish's. Gweneth thought of Ashley, the mirror in her room, steam billowing from the floor and the fireplace burning brightly, illuminating the entire room. Trish was completely motionless for the duration of the kiss, almost mesmerized by what she saw looking into Gweneth's eyes.

Gweneth could feel wetness between her own legs as she ended the kiss and broke eye contact. Trish blinked several times and looked like she could pass out. Gweneth put her arm around Trish and helped her sit down on the bed.

"Are you ok?" Gweneth asked.

"Yes. I'm fine, just a little disoriented. That's never happened to me before. What was that?" Trish responded.

"You asked what it was like, so I thought I'd show you rather than tell you. Do you feel any different?" Gweneth asked.

"I feel really tired. Is that normal?"

There was a quiet knock at the office suite door. Trish tried to stand, but still seemed too weak to move quick enough to get to the door without help.

"Stay here." Gweneth said as she proceeded into the office suite.

"You're not wearing any clothes." Trish indicated.

Gweneth turned and smiled, showing off her confidence.
"I know."

Gweneth looked through the peephole on the door and saw Joshua standing there, dressed business casual and carrying a leather briefcase. Gweneth opened the door and Joshua almost tripped over his own jaw walking into room 6015 as he noticed Gweneth standing there completely exposed and perfectly made.

Gweneth shut the door behind them and followed Joshua into the hotel suite. She started to feel more wetness between her legs and the urge to have him again was growing more intense with each step they took.

Joshua scanned the room then took a few steps into the bedroom suite, noticing Trish laying on the bed. Joshua was quickly at her side, checking her pulse.

"Is she ok?" Joshua asked. "What happened? Where's Susan?"

Gweneth tried to answer in the order the questions were asked. "I think she's fine. We kissed, like you and I did, eyes open, soft and delicate. It only lasted fifteen or twenty seconds and then she collapsed on the bed. She was awake or conscious when you knocked. Is she asleep?"

"She's passed out." Joshua turned to see Gweneth, still free of clothing or worry. "You tried to connect with her?"

"I did. Susan had to leave rather quickly. She had an issue of some kind she had to take care of. I think Susan and Trish were convinced I was Ashley. She took blood from my finger and then told me I'm moving into a house with housemates. That's about all I know."

Joshua seemed a little confused, however his attention was split between his initial concern for Trish and that Gweneth was still standing there, tempting his self control in more ways than one. Joshua needed separation for several seconds to breathe and focus his attention.

"Can you get a glass of water from the bathroom?" Joshua asked.

Gweneth returned to the bathroom she was in minutes before. She took the paper cover off a small water glass and filled the glass three quarters full. Gweneth's gaze creeped up to the mirror and there was her reflection, again with her eyes closed.
Gweneth saw a smile spread across her reflection's face and she

knew what was coming. Wanting to find out if she was right, Gweneth took a deep breath in through her nose and naturally made the same smile in the mirror. Gweneth's eyes were open, staring at Ashley's which were still closed. Instinctively, Gweneth leaned closer to the mirror.

Suddenly, Gweneth saw movement behind her then felt a hand on her shoulder. She quickly turned, startled, but didn't scream. Joshua held her naked body close at the waist but was leaning slightly backwards.

"Are you ok?"

"Yes, I'm…" Gweneth paused. "I'm…or I was about to transition again."
Gweneth took a moment to breathe, then continued. "I was trying earlier, when I first came upstairs, but Ashley was sleeping."

"Now she's wanting to wake up?"

"The kiss with Trish and you walking in, looking like a golf pro, but smelling really good." Gweneth pushed Joshua away. "I want you so bad right now." She sighed. "But I also want to sleep."

"I asked you to get water so I could have a few seconds to compose myself or I was going to make us both late." Joshua started walking back towards where Trish was laying, putting a little more distance between them. Trish was now awake with a strange look on her face.

Gweneth turned back towards the sink to grab the water and turn off the faucet when she caught a glance of Ashley in the mirror. She had the same smile on her face and her eyes were wide open.

CHAPTER 6

Monday, 4:27pm

"I'm ready." Gweneth said.

Susan stood up from her desk. "Gweneth, please follow me."

Susan walked out of her office and into the hall. Gweneth followed her towards an open door across the hall to room 6016, a lavish one bedroom suite with a balcony. The king bed in the bedroom was not made with standard hotel linen. It was more elegant and looked far more comfortable.
As Gweneth walked in she saw Trish holding a beautiful red dress which she held up to Gweneth's body, checking the size.

"Perfect." Trish said.

"Gweneth, now is a good time to cancel any plans you have for the evening, or for the next few months." Susan suggested.

"The next few months?" Gweneth questioned.

"If you pass the training requirements, you will begin working right away. There can be a steep learning curve and immersing yourself for the next few months is the best way to be successful." Susan faced Gweneth and looked in her eyes.

"I suggest telling your friends you've taken a new job on the west coast and won't be back until summer. Keep it short and sweet."

Gweneth took a few deep breaths and opened her cell phone. The screen read: No Service.
"Can I use the phone in here?" Gweneth asked. "I don't have

service inside.”

“You may.” Susan said. “Trish will explain your first training assignment for tonight. Welcome to the team and good luck.” Susan left the room and crossed the hall back into her office letting the door close behind her.

Gweneth used the phone on the desk just outside the bedroom. She called her friend Jessica with good and bad news. Taking Susan’s advice, Gweneth explained she did great on her interview but they need her to start immediately and they’re flying her to an office in Seattle. Jessica was happy for Gweneth and also disappointed they couldn’t hang out before she left. Gweneth asked her if she could call Molly, her other friend, and explain the situation. With promises to be in touch soon, Gweneth hung up the phone and started dialing Scott’s number but hung up after only pushing four digits. She didn’t want to break up with him over the phone and decided writing an email was less confrontational.

“Are you ready to learn about your first training assignment?” Trish asked, as she walked out of the bedroom.

“I am. Although, I’m nervous. This is all happening really fast.”

“Just remember to breathe.” Trish said walking into the living area of the suite. “Have a seat.”

Gweneth sat on the couch with both feet on the floor and her legs together, hands on her knees. Trish sat opposite Gweneth, in a chair that could easily fit two of her. Trish was 5’0 and 105lbs. Gweneth was a towering 5’4 and 121lbs.

“Do you remember Susan’s explanation of NLP or Neuro-Linguistic Programming?” Trish asked.

“I remember her explaining it, but I couldn’t define it at this point.”

"One of the world's leading experts on NLP is here in the hotel hosting a conference today and tomorrow. Your first training assignment tonight is to attend the reception and keynote address in the conference room downstairs. Because of the importance of NLP in our work, it's imperative that we work with the best of the best. Joshua Miller is by far the best. After his speech, watch him as he talks to the different types of people at the conference. When the right time presents itself, you are to approach Mr. Miller and engage in casual conversation with the undertone of flirting. Try to determine whether he's susceptible to influence through sex, money, or a different motivation."

Trish uncrossed and recrossed her legs the opposite direction. "You will have a cover story, as you should also mingle with other attendees. You are a journalist writing an article about people who benefit from NLP."

"That's it?" Gweneth asked. "That doesn't seem too difficult."

"Pay attention during the presentations so you have a frame of reference for later conversations. This is just the first test. Should you pass, there is a second part of the assignment you'll be briefed on after your meeting with Mr. Miller."

Trish stood up. "The presentation starts at 6:00pm so we need to get you ready. If you'd like to take a shower, we'll do your hair and makeup to match the event and the dress."

"Yeah, that sounds fine." Gweneth's voice sounded unsure. She stood and walked towards the bedroom. She stopped and turned toward Trish. "I actually brought an overnight bag with me with a change of clothes and make up. Can I run down to my car and grab it?"

Trish looked at Gweneth, assessing whether or not she would leave instead of retrieving her bag and returning to the hotel. "Go quickly!" Trish answered, testing Gweneth and herself.

Gweneth had her keys in her suit coat pocket and left the room, leaving her organizer behind. It didn't occur to Gweneth until she got on the elevator, that she could leave and escape back to her familiar call center job, friends, and sex life. Everything about this interview and opportunity seemed too good to be true or extremely far fetched. Sexual energy and NLP seemed strange and mythical, but the check for $20,000 was real.

Gweneth walked out the main entrance of the hotel lobby and was leaning towards leaving. 'I don't need that organizer.' She thought, as the idea of leaving grew. Instead of retrieving her bag from the back seat, she sat down in the driver seat and started her car. Gweneth sat for a moment, still not ready to leave.

The radio was playing an advertisement for a local law firm. Gweneth reached for the second pre-programed station on her radio when a new song started playing. It was a song Gweneth had heard numerous times and loved. "It's my Life" by Bon Jovi. As the song played she imagined her life as it could be, based on what little information she knew about Redhawk Marketing. She couldn't imagine her current life fitting to the lyrics or energy of the song.

Gweneth took a deep breath and remembered the breathing technique Susan had shown her. She closed her eyes and started breathing consciously and in rhythm. After only two minutes of conscious breathing Gweneth felt better and turned the engine off. She looked in the rearview mirror and took one more deep breath. "You got this." She said out loud to herself.

Gweneth grabbed her bag from the backseat and walked back in the lobby doors. She passed the same conference room that was marked with a Redhawk Marketing Group sign where she first met Trish. Gweneth stopped and opened the door on the right side. She was surprised to see a completely empty conference room. Further down the hall she saw people mingling in the hallway and going in and out of the restroom. She concluded that it was the NLP seminar and continued towards the elevators.

Gweneth approached the door to room 6016 and it opened before she could raise her hand to knock. Trish held the door as Gweneth walked in.
"I said go quickly!"

"Sorry. I...." Gweneth paused, "I forgot exactly where I parked."

"You don't need to lie. What made you decide to come back?" Trish responded calmer and with empathy, closing the door behind her.

Gweneth froze. "I'm sorry. I kinda panicked and yes, I did think of leaving."

"So what changed your mind?"

"I started breathing and calmed down." Gweneth smiled. "And Bon Jovi."

Trish thought for a moment. "Living on a Prayer?"

"It's my Life." Gweneth replied.

"That would have been my second guess. I can help you with your breathing and with practice you can be free of fear." Trish walked into the bathroom in the main bedroom and turned on the light. "But first, you need to shower and change. You have to be downstairs in thirty minutes."

Trish moved back into the bedroom letting Gweneth use the bathroom and shower. Gweneth set her bag on the counter and looked in the large mirror. Trish stood at the foot of the bed with her arms straight and hands together in front of her, almost like a bodyguard.

"Do you mind if I have a little privacy?" Gweneth asked.

"I'm here to help you get ready and help you move on to the next phase of training. You've wasted over fifteen minutes because you can't make up your mind quickly." Trish approached Gweneth and slowly touched her left elbow while looking her in the eyes. "Make a decision!" Trish snapped her fingers.

Gweneth slowly closed her eyes, and after several seconds, she slowly opened them. The reflection she saw in the mirror wasn't the same person. She had showered and was dressed in the red dress Trish had sized her with earlier, and her makeup and hair looked professionally done.

Gweneth took a shaky breath in, almost paralized. "What the fuck just happened?"

"You're back. Good." Trish was packing up Gweneth's clothes in her travel bag. "You're ready, and with nine minutes to spare."

"What happened? I just walked in the bathroom and now I'm ready?"

"I put you in a state of zero procrastination. You showered, dressed, did your makeup and hair, all in twenty-one minutes. See what you can accomplish if you don't overthink things." Trish was more relaxed, but showed little emotion.

"Why don't I remember getting ready? This is not what I expected." Gweneth had more anxiety than she was used to.

"You'll remember everything soon enough. Typically only lasts a few hours. Are you ready to head downstairs?"

"I'm not sure. I feel like I could be sick." Gweneth held her head over the sink.

"That's your anxiety and nerves settling. Take a few controlled breaths and when you feel comfortable, close your eyes." Trish moved to Gweneth's side.

Gweneth looked at her reflection and couldn't remember the last time she looked so pretty. She took several deep breaths, and made eye contact with Trish through her reflection in the mirror. Gweneth closed her eyes and continued her breathing pattern.

Trish spoke in a slower and more deliberate tone. She didn't touch Gweneth as she slowly moved from her right side to her left, speaking from behind her.

"I want you to continue breathing the same way and only focus on your breath. Feel life and energy traveling in and out of your body. The energy everywhere around us is all connected. When you breathe, you bring energy into your body, which magnifies your body's ability to create more energy."

Trish watched Gweneth's eyes in the mirror. She could tell by her eye movements that she was imagining something. Knowing she didn't have the time she would typically have, she sped up the process of finding Gweneth some confidence.

"I want you to imagine your perfect self. The version of you that has no fear, no inhibitions, and complete independence." Trish waited almost a minute before continuing. "This perfect woman has the confidence of a Queen, the heart of a nurse, and the eyes of an eagle. She is desired by everyone, and belongs to no one. She controls her universe with grace and style. She is not God, but a Goddess. Your Goddess." Trish paused again. Watching Gweneth's physical reactions she could tell her heartbeat was elevated. "Can you see her? Can you imagine a flawless version of yourself?"

Gweneth continued breathing and spoke intentionally, not reactionary.

"Yes. I can."

"Imagine how it would feel to be her. Don't imagine with your mind, imagine with your emotions. Everything you could ever want, you could have. You could hold any position in any company, help people who need help, and be who you were meant to be, because this whole universe is hers."

Gweneth began breathing harder and started taking breath in through her mouth. This was a sign to Trish that Gweneth was imagining a more perfect version of herself, which was increasing her arousal. Her eyes were moving a bit faster and her pulse continued to increase.

Trish whispered in Gweneth's left ear, "Use your senses to remember her. What does she smell like? How soft is her skin? How deep are her eyes?"
Trish then extended her right arm and held her hand behind Gweneth's head. She extended her left arm and held her hand just above Gwenth's left shoulder, then continued. "What does her voice sound like? What's her name?"

Gweneth took a deeper breath in and exhaled, "Ashley."

Trish then firmly grasped Gweneth's left shoulder and pulled down. The force was not hard enough to move Gweneth's feet, but she did become weak in the knees and started to fall backwards. Trish cradled Gweneth's neck and head with her right hand and gently guided Gweneth to the bathroom floor with her left arm. Gweneth's eyes were still moving behind her eyelids and her breathing and pulse had slowed. Trish held Gweneth's head and pressed gently on the middle of her forehead with both her thumbs. Trish closed her eyes and took several deep and focused breaths, exhaling slowly, blowing energy from her body into Gweneth's.
Trish brushed Gweneth's hair behind her ear.

"I don't know if I should say I'm sorry or you're welcome." She whispered, then speaking her name, intending to wake her up. "Gwen. Gwen."

Gweneth opened her eyes. "What happened?"

"You fainted." Trish answered.

Gweneth took a deep breath. "What does that mean?"

"Nothing bad. Your nervous system has just had a little more stimulation than normal. Do you feel like you can stand up?"

Gweneth took one more deep breath and nodded. Trish helped her rise from the bathroom floor and made sure Gweneth felt stable. "How do you feel?"

"Ok, just a little dazed. I don't think I've ever fainted before."

"Take a few deep breaths and when you're ready, I'll walk you to the elevator."

Gweneth looked at her reflection in the mirror and started to feel better. She took several breaths and pulled her hair back into a ponytail and secured it with a hair tie. 'Better.' She thought. Gweneth walked out of the bathroom and met Trish by the door.

"Do you remember your cover story?" Trish asked.

"I'm a journalist writing an article on how NLP has benefited people. I should mingle and make contact with Mr. Miller - the keynote speaker. I need to determine what his motivations are. Question. If I'm a journalist, who do I work for?"

"How about the University of Miami? A journalism student won't be as polished and should you run into any other members of the press, it's a plausible reason why they haven't heard of you. I think you should use an alias. Get into character."

"I could use my middle name. Ashley." Gweneth suggested.

"Perfect!" Trish responded, showing rare enthusiasm. She handed Gweneth a small red strapless purse which matched her dress and shoes. Gweneth didn't notice her Valentino heels until she was several steps out the door making her way down the hall. If she had known she was wearing $600 on each foot she might have fainted a second time.

Gweneth pressed the down arrow for the elevator and waited patiently. She focused on her breath as she looked at her reflection in the glass of the elevator doors. She didn't feel nervous or worried, rather excited and confident. She practiced introducing herself by repeating the name Ashley so it sounded natural. "Hi, I'm Ashley." Gweneth said. "I'm Ashley, nice to meet you. My name is Ashley, what's yours?"

The elevator doors opened and Gweneth stepped in, selecting the button for the Lobby. The doors closed and she continued introducing herself. Each time she repeated her middle name her confidence grew. The elevator stopped on the second floor and Gweneth stood back to let a man and a young boy step on. They were dressed in swimming trunks and tee shirts and the boy had goggles dangling around his neck.

He looked at Gweneth and smiled. "We're going swimming!" "That sounds like fun!" Gweneth replied. She looked at the boy's father who looked to be in his late twenties. "He's adorable." Gweneth smiled, referring to his son.

The boy's father froze for several seconds. It seemed he didn't know what to say or how to react to a normal complement. "Thank you."

"I'm Ashley." Gweneth said, extending her hand. The elevator stopped and the doors opened.

"I'm taking my son to the pool." The man replied, following his son off the elevator, blushing and flushed with sudden anxiety. They hurried off around the corner, the man looking back at Gweneth twice before they disappeared from sight. Even though the interaction was off, Gweneth felt like she knew why and was flattered.

Before the presentation started, Gweneth found herself standing towards the back of the large conference room, observing the other people in attendance. She noticed business men dressed in suits, many already in conversation. There were fewer women than men and Gweneth didn't see anyone close to her own age. She noticed a woman she thought to be in her late twenties or early thirties. This woman stood out because of her distinct voice. It was a higher pitch than most women and was easy to recognize in almost any setting. She was the same height as Gweneth, but a few pounds heavier. She was also one of the few attendees who came in casual attire wearing blue jeans and a University of Arizona sweatshirt. Gweneth decided she would be the first person she'd approach and she walked over to where she was standing.

"Hi." Gweneth said, keeping it casual.

"Hi. I'm Kathy." She introduced herself with a smile and offered a friendly wave rather than a handshake.

"Ashley." Gweneth replied. "What brings you to an NLP seminar?" Kathy started a semi-rehearsed monologue about the last few years of her life, living with extreme OCD and Bi-polar disorder. She explained how six months of NLP techniques have helped her more than three years of pharmacopeia.
Gweneth listened and was interested in her progress. A short, balding man in his late thirties walked up and smiled, making solid eye contact with Gweneth.
"Thank you for coming. I'm Paul Johnson, Mr. Miller's business partner and workshop coach." Paul extended his hand. "I see you've met Kathy."

Gweneth shook his hand and smiled, returning the eye contact. "I'm Ashley." She felt a bit awkward not offering a last name. She didn't want to show any hesitation and continued. "Kathy told me her story and it's very interesting."

"Six months ago Kathy couldn't or wouldn't leave her apartment, paralyzed with two debilitating disorders. After a two month plan of eliminating most of her medication and starting weekly programming sessions, she was able to go back to work and function comfortably in most public settings."

"That's incredible." Gweneth smiled at Kathy. "Congratulations."

Kathy offered a shy, "Thank you."

"What brings you to the seminar, Ashley?" Paul asked.

"I'm a journalism student and have been curious about Neuro-Linguistic Programming and thought I would attend to help me decide if it's a story I want to pursue."

"Exciting. What other research have you done?"

"Not much. I have plans to meet a friend on the beach side and thought this was too good of an opportunity to pass up."

"It's a pleasure to meet you Ms. Ashley. Please let me know if I can answer any questions for you." Paul shook her hand and presented her with a business card.

"Thank you. It was nice meeting you." Gweneth took the business card and put it in her purse. She then looked at Kathy.
"Kathy, it was nice to meet you too. I'm excited to learn what's made your improvement possible."

Gweneth walked back towards the back of the room where she entered. Even though she felt good she also was starting to feel a bit of anxiety. She had never blatantly lied to strangers before. It wasn't something she was comfortable with. Gweneth picked up a bottled water from a table with an unimpressive offering of complimentary beverages. Her other choices included coffee or apple juice. The thought of a long island iced tea jumped into Gweneth's mind which led to thoughts of her original plan of meeting her friends for drinks.

She took a few deep breaths, focusing on her objective and her confident self. "I can do this." She whispered, taking a sip of water. She visually scanned the large conference room and noticed several pairs of eyes casually looking her direction and then casually looking away. Gweneth decided to walk the room and observe. It took her eight minutes to slowly walk from one side of the room to the other, occasionally stopping, sitting, moving, and listening.

The lights in the large room dimmed twice signaling that the presentation was about to start. The Master of Ceremonies was a middle aged man who had a deep voice which made his presents seem larger than it was. He told two jokes few people understood and even fewer laughed at. He introduced the first speaker as Gweneth found a seat towards the back of the room. After a few minutes of breathing Gweneth became focused on every word.

•   •   •   •

Trish walked off the elevator on the first floor and headed towards the NLP conference. She had changed her clothes, now dressed like a hotel employee, and carried a small zippered daytimer. She turned to her right and walked down a hallway which had access to the service staff, a dressing room, and private restrooms for VIPs. She fastened a name tag to her jacket and approached the main dressing room, knocking on the door. She blocked the eye hole with her palm and suddenly the door opened. Joshua Miller stood in the doorway with a look of shock on his face.

"What are you doing here?"

"We need to talk. Quickly." Trish responded, stepping into the room and Joshua closing the door behind her. "We have a very small window and I need you for a ritual tonight."

"What! There's no way I can do anything tonight." Joshua was irritated and sat down on a small sofa in the corner of the room.

"Susan recruited a new girl who is somewhat remarkable. Her energy is incredibly high and her focus is stronger than any other recruit I've worked with. This is the girl we've been waiting for." Trish was unemotional and strictly business.

"I don't think it's possible tonight." Joshua raised his hand to his head and ran his fingers through his hair. "I have a huge workshop tomorrow and can't miss it. Can we start the ritual tomorrow night?"

"Susan is lining up an assignment for this Friday and will have this young woman ready, with or without your help. She has a programmer ready to do this, however if we lose this girl, it could be six months before we get another chance." Trish paused and looked Joshua in the eyes. "This was your idea. You said we needed someone on the inside, who is loyal to us and aware enough to help."

"I know that's what I said. I still believe that. I just don't think we're ready. If we rush it and make a mistake, we're both as good as dead."

"I think this girl is worth the risk."

"Not now. Not yet."

Trish was getting frustrated with Joshua's unwillingness to budge. "What if you meet her before you decide?"

"I've already decided and you know there shouldn't be any contact before a ritual like this."

"I think we're making a mistake, not taking advantage of this opportunity when it's in our grasp."

"I'm on stage in a few minutes. Is there anything else you need right now?" Joshua asked, growing tired of Trish's persistence.

"I will let Susan know to move forward with the other Programmer and let you get on with your presentation." Trish turned and walked toward the door. "Just to let you know, she's in the audience. I'll bet you can identify her before you get off stage."

"There's three hundred people in there and you think I'll be able to pick her out from the stage, in under thirty minutes, while presenting?" Joshua chuckled. "Your confidence in me is flattering, but even if that's the case, there's still no way I can do anything until tomorrow night or Wednesday."

"I guess we'll never know." Trish left the suite without a cordial goodbye, just a smug look of indifference. Joshua didn't know Trish was expecting him to turn down the opportunity and that she had other ideas. She needed him to know that there was someone in the audience who was a top candidate. Knowing Joshua as she does, Trisha knew he would now be looking for her.

•   •   •   •

Gweneth paid attention for the whole two hour presentation and watched how other people reacted to each presenter. When Joshua Miller walked on stage, she recognized his name from the introduction, and her focus was now on the keynote speaker. His voice was deeper than she expected, and his movements on stage were minimal. He narrated two powerpoint presentations, showing the effectiveness of certain NLP treatments. The clinical and more scientific information went over Gweneth's head, however she noticed several people taking notes and absorbing the information far better than her. She assumed they were medical or psychiatric professionals.
Towards the end of Joshua's speech he made eye contact with Gweneth. At first she thought he was just looking out into the room, but after close to a minute, she realized he was looking her in the eyes from over a hundred feet away. 'Does he know about me?' She wondered.

After Joshua finished his presentation he was mingling with different people and small groups within the conference room. He answered questions while shaking hands and thanking people for attending. Gweneth found herself in a casual conversation with two business men who found her attractive. They were flirting and Gweneth flirted back as she was keeping an eye on Joshua. One of them mentioned knowing Mr. Miller and Gweneth was quick to request an introduction. Within a few minutes, the man returned with Joshua just two steps behind him.

"Ashley, this is Joshua Miller. Mr. Miller, this is Ashley. She's a journalism student."

"Nice to meet you." Gweneth said, extending her hand.

"Ashley, it's nice to meet you as well." Joshua shook her hand, then immediately looked into her eyes, somewhat shocked at what he felt.
"What did you think of the presentation?"

"Honestly, I didn't understand everything, but I'm still learning the basics of NLP. I find it fascinating, which is why I'm just getting started with preliminary research."

"Thank you for coming. Let my assistant Paul know if there's any information we can give you." Joshua replied with a generic response and now trying to avoid eye contact.

"Actually, I was hoping I could get just a few minutes of your time to ask a few questions I have. Can we grab a drink in the bar?" Gweneth was surprised at how confident she felt asking a complete stranger to the bar for a drink.

"I have a few more people I'd like to say hello to and then I'll be at the reception. Find me there and I'll give you a few minutes." Joshua said, excusing himself and moving on to the next small group.

Gweneth thanked the business men for introducing her and moved on. She continued to introduce herself as Ashley and had a few casual conversations before the conference room was almost empty. The entire time she watched Joshua. She paid attention to his movements, his facial expressions, and body language. He never looked in her direction, or made eye contact since their introduction.

Joshua left the conference room and Gweneth followed him, lagging far enough behind as not to be suspected of following him. Gweneth passed the front desk, drawing the attention of a young man working and the guest he was checking into the hotel. She made her way to the restaurant which was crowded for a Monday night. There was a patio bar and private dining balcony which sat forty guests comfortably. There were attendees from the conference along with staff and investors. The reception was casual and offered an open bar, which many patrons took advantage of.

Gweneth spotted Joshua drinking a glass of red wine while mingling with colleagues and friends. She continued to watch him and noticed his confidence and lack of ego as he spoke casually and carried on conversations with ease.

Joshua turned and spotted Gweneth observing the room. He walked over and re-introduced himself. "You are Ashley, correct?"

Almost correcting him, but catching herself, she managed to exhale, "Na,…actually, yes. Sorry. Ashley. Not Actually. Wow, I should be better at this." Gweneth was caught off guard with Joshua's sudden interest in her.
"I enjoyed your presentation earlier." Gweneth said feeling a different topic other than her name would help her focus.

"Thank you. How much of it did you understand?"

"Not as much as I expected to, but enough to have a foundation for developing a few ideas." Gweneth felt as if she was trying to keep her head above the waterline. She felt very transparent and feared that Joshua could see through her facade.

"I have a few minutes before we start the reception. It might be a few hours before I could give you the same time once the speeches start, and you don't want to stay for this stuff."

"Sounds good." Gweneth replied, smiling. "Where should we sit?"

"Follow me." Joshua led her to the private dining balcony and sat at a small, unoccupied table. "What questions can I answer for you?" He asked as they sat down.

"Can you tell me a little more about yourself?" Gweneth asked.

Joshua was uncomfortable with the question thinking most journalists do a little research before they attend a conference on something, but answered the question vaguely.
"I have two Masters Degrees. The first from Harvard, and the second from a University in India. I've been studying hypnosis and different ways of communicating with the subconscious as well as neurology, psychology, and sociology. I started developing this new NLP system five years ago and so far we've had tremendous success."

"What was school like in India? That must have been an interesting experience." Gweneth, having not given much thought to the questions she would ask, was trying to start a more social conversation. Joshua was starting to pick up on the cues Gweneth was giving off.

"India was amazing. I was there for three years. I'm sorry, what does this have to do with your article on NLP?"

Gweneth was put on the spot and lost focus. "It doesn't. Not really. You surprised me and I hadn't prepared any questions yet." Her heart was pounding and she was sure he could hear it thumping in her chest. "I thought I'd take the few minutes I have and get to know the man behind the system."

Gweneth locked eyes with Joshua and gave a shy smile. He didn't say a word. He sat across from Gweneth and engaged in a short staring contest. Gweneth became self-conscious after the first fifteen seconds and looked down.

"Ashley, you seem very nice, but I have guests and a reception to get back to. I appreciate your interest. If you'd like a quote for your article, call Paul Johnson and he can get something for you." Joshua stood up from the table while Gweneth remained seated.

"I'm sorry I wasted your time." Gweneth said, obviously

disappointed in herself. She felt as if she had just failed her first test and would probably have to give back the $20,000 check.

"Have a good night. Ashley?" Joshua couldn't resist asking her name one more time. He knew she was not a student or journalist and was certain this was the girl Trish had told him about earlier. He was just as certain her name was not Ashley. She sat in silence and didn't respond. Joshua walked away disappointed and annoyed, not with Gweneth, but with Trish.

Gweneth sat in silence when she heard someone inside start to give a speech, thanking Joshua and his team. She stood up from the table and walked inside. She tried to hold her head high and walk as if she didn't feel defeated. As she neared the front of the restaurant she heard Joshua's voice addressing the small crowd. Gweneth turned and watched for only a moment before she heard a familiar voice behind her.

"Didn't go so well?" The voice asked.

Gweneth turned suddenly. "Trish. Hi. Ah, no. I think I crashed and burned. I don't even think he believed my name was Ashley."

"It's ok. I didn't expect you to get much information. Just the fact that you tried and were able to get a few minutes alone with him was enough to pass the first test."

"What? Really?" Gweneth's natural optimism was peeking through the clouds.

"Let's get you upstairs and ready for the second and more important test." Trish gave her a small, reassuring smile. "You'll do better in the next phase. The playing field will be a little more even."

Unsure of what to expect next, Gweneth followed Trish back to the elevator, reminding her of when she first arrived at the hotel six hours before.

• • • •

Gweneth walked into the same room she had changed in, however this time, the room was lit with candles, soft chimes, and trance like music. An incense was burning and smelled familiar and potent.

"Take your shoes off and lay on the bed." Trish stated.

Gweneth only hesitated for a second but then slipped off the designer shoes she was wearing and proceeded to the bedroom. She laid on her back with her arms at her sides. Trish turned up the volume of the music and lit another candle that burned a larger flame. Trish sat in a chair at the foot of the bed, both feet on the floor and with perfect posture. Trish started breathing in a specific pattern.

"Close your eyes." Trish said. Gweneth followed her instruction and hadn't said a word since entering the hotel room.

Trish continued breathing in rhythm and started a guided meditation for Gweneth. Her objective was to put Gweneth in a deep enough hypnotic state that she could bring out her imagined perfect version of herself, eliminating fear, anxiety, and her lack of confidence. She needed Gweneth to try to seduce Joshua in his room which could only happen if Gweneth had the confidence to pounce and Joshua had his mind opened enough to see the opportunity in front of him.

Over the next three hours Trish had Gweneth breathing and focused on her perfect self. Trish knew the effects and changes Gweneth would experience would only be temporary and last an hour or two at most. The phone in the hotel room rang and Trish answered it within two rings. The call was very short, less than ten seconds. Timing was very important from this point forward. Trish brought Gweneth out of the meditation and tested her work.

"What's your name?"

"Ashley. What's going on? Where am I?"

"You're right where you're supposed to be." Trish answered. "You're ready to meet Mr. Miller. You'll wait for him in his room, free as a bird, and as patient as a lioness watching her prey."
She gave Gweneth instructions and a hotel room key to room 5015.
"Lay naked on the bed and keep breathing. There is a pack of cigarettes in your purse. If you feel the need, smoke one or two to keep your breathing pattern consistent and relaxed."

Trish opened the hotel room door. "You're ready Ashley." Gweneth stood up from the bed and stepped into the same shoes she was wearing before. She picked up her small purse and followed Trish down the hall to the bank of elevators. Both stepped into the same elevator and Trish pushed the buttons for the fifth floor and the Lobby.

• • • •

Expecting that Gweneth wouldn't have any problems letting herself into Joshua's room, Trish took the elevator to the ground floor and had a smile waiting for Joshua when the elevator doors opened. He looked tired and was headed to his room to get some sleep. When he saw Trish his exhaustion level seemed to double. Joshua stood there, contemplating whether or not to get on the elevator.
Joshua stepped on and locked eyes with Trish. He didn't say anything and didn't select any button or turn to face the closing doors. Instead, after the doors shut, he smiled and gave Trish a strong hug. He then stood back and locked eyes with her again.

"Really?" Joshua smirked. "You had her wear that dress? She stood out like a butterfly in a room full of moths."

Trish lowered her head for a moment. She did this, not as a sign of weakness or apology, but rather a form of submission and respect.

She lifted her head and returned a similar smile. "What do you think?"

Joshua took in a deeper than normal breath and let out an apologetic sigh. "I agree with you. She's a very good candidate, but there is still nothing I can do this evening. Can Susan possibly wait until tomorrow night?"

It was Trish's turn to take a deep breath and sigh. "Unfortunately, we don't have a choice. I already told Susan you would do it and the programmer has been reassigned. You are the only one who can attempt this with a good chance of success. Your room has already been prepared, and scoped.

"I can't believe you'd put me in this position. I can't abandon the workshop tomorrow and I can't be in two places at once."

"I do have a solution that solves all dilemmas in this situation, however you won't like it."

"There is only one solution and that is to find a reason, any reason, to postpone just one night. I will be happy and eager to start our deception and take down this company, but it has to wait twenty hours or so."

"My solution is a little different, and it's effective almost immediately." Trish reached around Joshua and pushed the button for the tenth floor and the elevator started moving.

Joshua turned around and looked at the button and asked, "Why are we going to ten?"

Trish extended a small syringe from her coat sleeve and inserted it into Joshua's butt cheek while his back was turned. She quickly pushed the contents of the syringe into Joshua's body.

"What the HELL!" Joshua yelled.

"I'm sorry, and I hope you forgive me." Trish started to explain. "I can explain in more detail later, but this is why I'm in the position

I'm in. I take risks to make sure things get done. I couldn't do what I'm about to do without a little help from our friend here." Trish showed Joshua the syringe which was familiar to him. "I'm going to induce a mild hypnosis and you are going to get this girl on our side, tonight."

"You might have ruined our chances before we've even started." Joshua's tone was slower and somber. Trish took his wrist and checked his pulse. Despite his initial reaction, Joshua's heart rate was slowing down and effects of the drug running through his veins made him susceptible to suggestion.

The elevator arrived at the tenth floor and Trish pulled the emergency stop button. Joshua was over a foot taller than Trish and to make the next part of her plan work, she needed to see Joshua's eyes.

"I want you to get on your knees." Trish stated.

Joshua started to kneel. "I'm only doing this to beg you not to do what I think you're going to do."

Trish looked deep into Joshua's eyes and gave another command. "I want you to keep your arms at your sides." Trish held Joshua's face in both of her small hands, still gazing deeper into Joshua's eyes.
"I want you to want to help this girl. I want you to help her become the woman she wants be. She is strong and deserving of the chance." Trish dropped her arms to her side and took a step back. "Close your eyes."

Joshua followed her instructions.

"When the elevator doors open you will walk to your room, expecting to go to bed. Half way down the hallway you will reach for your room key and drop the contents of your pocket, revealing a note. The ritual you will perform you've known was coming. Paul can handle the workshop on his own. You will not remember any of our conversations from today until the next time you wake."

Trish pushed the elevator stop button back in and pressed the button for the fifth floor.

"She has already been prepped and is in a goddess-like state. Her real name will lift the hypnosis so you can begin. Open your eyes and stand up."

Joshua followed instructions once again. Trish continued while putting a folded piece of paper in his right left pants pocket. "You just finished the reception and are headed to your room."

Just like that the elevator doors opened and Joshua stepped out. He turned and looked back at the elevator and didn't see Trish at all, but something told him he wasn't expecting to. Joshua started slowly walking down the hallway to his room, thinking only about how exhausted he felt.

CHAPTER 7

Wednesday, 5:28am

Gweneth awoke in her 1993 Honda Civic dazed and disoriented. She felt as if she had taken a nap but she didn't remember falling asleep. Even stranger for Gweneth, it didn't seem to bother her. She knew she was in the parking lot of the Ritz Carlton South Beach. Thinking she fell asleep for only a few minutes, Gweneth checked her reflection in the rearview mirror and brushed her bangs back behind her ear. Gweneth knew she looked tired and the idea of going to sleep was the greatest idea of all time. Gweneth looked forward, not noticing her reflection's eyes still staring directly back at her. She started her car and almost froze in place.

For a moment, Gweneth felt paralyzed, and again, she didn't panic or seemed worried. She shifted her eyes to the clock radio which read, 5:28 and within a fraction of a second changed to 5:29.

Joshua's words repeated in Gweneth's head. It's all she could focus on. His voice penetrated her mind in a way that was romantic and very persuasive.

"Deposit the check in the ATM on Broadway. Read the note in your pocket then and put it somewhere you're sure to find it. Drive home and drink every sip of orange juice on the way. Go straight to your bed and sleep."

Joshua's dialogue looped, over and over. Gweneth's clock radio on her dashboard turned from 5:29 to 5:30. Immediately Gweneth put her car in gear and exited the hotel parking lot.

She quickly found her way onto the A1A Highway, parallel to the Atlantic Ocean. After several miles Gweneth turned on Broadway Ave and continued west until she reached the bank Joshua had referred to. There was no one in line this early in the morning and Gweneth pulled right up to the ATM. She completed the deposit slip, and signed the check Susan had given her, not realizing the immediate significance of that amount of money. The ATM accepted the envelope from Gweneth and returned her ATM card along with a receipt, showing a $20,000.00 deposit, pending.
With no one behind her, Gweneth took the note from her left jacket pocket and unfolded the first crease. She read the three most important things in her life, breathing between each one. There was a second crease in the note, however she did not feel compelled to unfold it any further.

Gweneth refolded the note and noticed the headlights of another car behind her. She lowered her sunshade and left the folded note and the ATM receipt tucked away as she flipped the visor up and pulled out of the bank parking lot. The morning traffic was starting to build in volume and Gweneth knew she'd be home in less than ten minutes.

She picked up the bottled orange juice in her cup holder and started drinking after a few shakes. It didn't taste like orange juice, but it also didn't taste like anything else. Gweneth realized that she didn't taste anything at all. The more she thought about it, the more curious she became and drank more and more of the juice until it was gone. She only worried about her sense of taste until she arrived home, minutes later.

Gweneth parked in her normal parking spot and went over the instructions in her head, completing a mental checklist. She looked at the clock which read 5:59am. The sun was beginning to break on the horizon but the typical glare wasn't as harsh this morning with dissipating thunderstorms, several miles off the east coast.

Gweneth was trying to remember what day it was or what had happened to her. Her memory was fuzzy and her eyelids were becoming extremely heavy.

The last few words Joshua said repeated in her head.
"Once home, go straight to your bed and sleep."

Gweneth turned off her car and carried her gym bag to the front door. She turned around, as she always does, and clicked a button, activating her car alarm. A large seabird squalled above her and Gweneth looked up to see the bird soaring with blue sky above, heading back to sea.

She smiled and thought to herself, 'I hope I dream of soaring among the clouds.' Her head spinning and unsure if this was even her apartment, Gweneth turned the key and went inside.

She closed the door, took five steps to her queen size bed and fell into a deep comatose like slumber.

To be continued....

Eyes Open

Available Fall 2022

Inner Goddess

Winter 2022

About the Author:

AJ Bradley was raised and currently resides in Colorado. After years of writing as a hobby, AJ is very proud to publish the OSM Origin Series starting with Book One: First Breath. The series continues with **Book Two: Eyes Open, and Book Three: Inner Goddess.**
AJ has enjoyed writing for over twenty-five years and has several other projects to be published in the coming years.

"48 Jobs and Counting" - 2023/2024

A collection of memoirs sharing memories and experiences accrued over twenty years of working in the service industry.

"Our Sexual Manifesto: Erin & Alex"
2024/2025

The series continues with the orginal characters in the OSM Series. This project is currently being developed as a web series, promoting sensual and sexual education for modern times.

When not writing AJ enjoys spending time with family and friends. AJ also finds peace in playing golf, flying airplanes, and performing at open mic nights.

In 2020, AJ created a Podcast and media company. RoseGarden Media, LLC launched **"The Long Way Around with Aaron Bradley"**. Season one is available for download now! Season two - TBD.

RoseGardenMedia.com
abradley@rosegardenmedia.com

Copyright 2022 - RoseGarden Media, LLC